HUSH

HUSH

EVA KONSTANTOPOULOS

authorHOUSE®

AuthorHouse™
1663 Liberty Drive
Bloomington, IN 47403
www.authorhouse.com
Phone: 1-800-839-8640

Published by AuthorHouse 6/5/2015

ISBN: 978-1-4685-0291-6 (sc)
ISBN: 978-1-4685-0292-3 (e)

Certain stock imagery © Thinkstock.
Any people depicted in stock imagery provided by Thinkstock are models, and such images are being used for illustrative purposes only.

Original Cover Design: Matthew Blom
Original Photo: Andrea Konstantopoulos

Print information available on the last page.

It is wonderful that five thousand years have now elapsed since the creation of the world, and still it is undecided whether or not there has ever been an instance of the spirit of any person appearing after death. All argument is against it; but all belief is for it.

Samuel Johnson, quoted by James Boswell

The dream is always the same. It's just a trickle at first, dark hallways, empty rooms, but then I see a face. Eyes wide, nostrils flaring, a little girl's mouth covered with tape. The room is damp and cold and simple, a chair in the middle of it all. That's where the girl sits in a yellow dress, hands bound and feet dangling off the floor.

I want to tell the girl to run, to fight back, to scream, but I can't move my lips. I can only watch as a hand strips off the tape over the girl's mouth and picks up a pair of pliers, the hand tilting the girl's head back and prying her mouth open. The pliers reach down, pulling on the girl's tongue, stretching it longer and longer, the walls closing in and the girl's eyes pleading...

"Freak!"

I sit up in the back seat and look out the window. Our client's not here yet. Thank God. We're parked on a quaint residential street a few miles from campus. Although this is the third house we've done and we're getting into a routine, I still feel guilty about our little business.

Jackson, my big brother, grins at me from the driver's seat. "You really got to stop talking in your sleep."

"I wasn't," I say, feeling saliva running down my cheek. *Crap.* I look over to Elliot, who fiddles with an EMF meter next to me. He smiles politely and I wipe the drool from my face. *Classy, Angela. Really classy.*

"That same dream again?" Elliot asks.

I nod. "Maybe it's a sign."

"Bullshit," Jackson quickly chimes in. "You're just not sleeping. It's those pills. You need to get off them."

"She's had the same dream for months," Elliot says.

Jackson's girlfriend, Beth, turns around in the front seat. Her blonde, silky hair cascades around her face. She could be a model if she wasn't so obsessed with my brother. "Maybe you should go see someone?" she says.

"Yeah, because she's loaded." Jackson rolls his eyes. My brother, like my father, would rather die by firing squad than go to any kind of shrink. It's partly my mother's fault. She was such a believer in things that go bump in the night, my father spent most of our childhood trying to prove her wrong. "Remember what we talked about, Ange," Jackson says. "It's all in your head. Best thing for you would be to quit. Cold turkey."

A low ache wraps around my rib cage. When my mother was alive she used to call my recurring dreams premonitions. She'd always tell me to keep a dream journal to watch out for patterns, but I never could get myself to write in one. I wanted my dreams to stay in my head. Committing them to paper made the images more real.

"You have to admit," Jackson says. "Lately, you've been nervous. More than usual."

I don't say anything. I'm not sure how to react, because he's right. Jackson glances at me in the rear view mirror. "We need to stop hiding," he says.

"So, you too?" I say. Jackson may not be on meds, but I know he has a secret stash of all kinds of fun stuff back home: oxy, booze, grass, snuff…

"Sure, Ange." Jackson grips the steering wheel. "I guess. But you're my main concern. Have you slept this week?"

I haven't, but I don't see what that has to do with anything.

"After this gig then, we should try it. I'm just saying."

"Maybe."

"Those pills have never been good for you. Maybe they helped a little growing up, with all that was going on, with Mom's condition and going broke. It's time. To move forward."

Beth places a hand on his thigh. He smiles at her.

"I'll think about it," I say, and I mean it. I really will. The truth is I'm terrified about going off them, but I'd never tell Jackson that. He thinks fear is for the weak.

A blue volkswagon pulls up in the driveway and a sixty-something man wearing a plaid shirt gets out of the driver's seat. Jackson flashes his trademark smile, all charisma and white teeth. "Mr. Hampton. It's a pleasure to meet you."

Mr. Hampton returns Jackson's smile with a timid upturn of his lips. "You the ghost catching people?" he asks.

"That's right. As you requested," Jackson replies.

"Well, you better come in then."

Mr. Hampton opens the door to his house. He walks

slowly up the stairs, deep rings of sweat under his armpits. "I knew I never should have stayed here after she died," he says. "Millie was never satisfied. Should have known death wouldn't be any different."

"Millie…?"

"Oh, my wife," he says, wiping a thick handkerchief across his forehead. "She was always stomping her feet, thumping her cane on the wall, and now she keeps doing it, pacing back and forth, rocking in her chair. Haven't been able to sleep."

"Can we look around?" Elliot says. He leans forward, listening intently. To be honest, I'm surprised Elliot and Jackson are even friends, let alone *best* friends. Elliot's the sensitive one. The one who always shows up when he says he will, who doesn't say much, but when he does, you can tell he's chosen his words carefully.

Mr. Hampton seems to stall at Elliot's request. Jackson takes over. "It would help if you show us where you've come in contact with Millie," he says.

"Of course." Mr. Hampton takes us around the living room, pointing out where he heard the knock, by the fireplace. There, and then again. I take notes. Sometimes I make diagrams. Draw pictures. Anything to keep my hands busy so I don't have to look Mr. Hampton in the eyes.

He leads us into the kitchen. "Here, in this little door, I heard some scraping, then banging. Knew it was Millie just by the thwacks. She always liked knocking that cane around. Letting me know what was what."

Elliot bends down and glances through the cupboard. There's a small hole in the back. He hangs back with me as Mr. Hampton and the others go ahead. "Probably some animal in the walls. Running around. Starving for food," he says, his voice low.

"Nothing we can't handle," I reply, trying not to show how nervous I am. Mr. Hampton looks back at us.

"This is a nice old house, mister," Elliot says to Mr. Hampton. He runs his hands along the wall. "Good bones."

Mr. Hampton smiles. "Lived here all my life. Don't know anything else."

He takes us up the ladder to the attic. A couple of rats scurry against the wall. Other than that though, there's just cobwebs, cardboard boxes, lots of dust. We balance on the wooden beams. Elliot helps me down the ladder, wrapping his arms around my waist and lowering me gently to the floor.

After surveying the whole house and detailing all the places Millie has made contact, Mr. Hampton stands by the sink, washing his hands and drying them with a damp washcloth. "So, how are you going to do it?" he asks.

Although this is our third gig and we've rehearsed this moment, I find myself frozen, smiling dumbly at our customer. Thankfully, Jackson jumps in. "Mr. Hampton, do you have family you can stay with?" he asks. "It's best if we investigate the house overnight. Ghosts are more receptive in the nocturnal hours. They can be rather shy during the day."

"I can go to my daughter's, I suppose," he says, a bit hesitant.

"It's just better for the occupant to lay low and let us do our thing. We will, of course, provide video footage of any contact we have with Millie. In case she wants to say her farewells," Jackson says.

"It's also safer," Beth says. "For you. Less emotional this way."

"You're the experts," Mr. Hampton says. "She's probably tired of having me around anyway."

He stands oafishly by the door.

This is wrong, wrong, wrong, I think. I look to Elliot to make sure he agrees with me. He shifts from foot to foot, but doesn't say anything.

Mr. Hampton hands over the keys. Jackson takes them with a little bow. As the old man leaves, he rests a hand on the wooden doorframe. "Take care, my love," he says. "Sleep tight."

When Mr. Hampton shuts the door, we don't do anything at first. Everyone stands still, studying the old man's living room. I plop down on the couch. "Can't believe it worked *again*," I say.

"I know," Elliot replies.

"Of course it works. We're pros," Jackson says.

"Next time this might be more efficient if we have them stay," Beth says, hooking up the computer equipment.

"You think?" Jackson asks.

"Definitely. Get in, get out. Then we spend less time with the wackos."

Jackson kisses Beth. "Revise. Rinse. Repeat." He claps his hands together. "Alright then. Let's get to work."

I lift the window curtain and peer out into the driveway. Mr. Hampton sits in his car, staring off into space. Elliot sidles up next to me. We watch him start the car and slowly reverse, backing out onto the street.

"Let's go, Ange," Jackson says. "Vamanos."

Elliot takes out the cameras one by one. I pick up the EMF meter. Jackson studies my face. "Beth, let's get some more make-up on my sis. Cover up the bags under her eyes."

"I can do it," I say.

"You want to borrow some stuff?" Beth asks. She pulls out her arsenal of eye shadows, creams and glosses.

"No. I got it."

I use the window to apply some concealer. Then I set up candles and place a pendant around my neck. Jackson says it's important to properly accessorize when on camera. The pendant is my mother's, though she hardly wore it. She liked to be free of jewelry, that way the spirits wouldn't have anything to latch onto, but little bells and whistles like pendants tend to put our customers at ease.

Jackson turns out the lights. I watch the candle flames cast long shadows along the walls.

"Don't just stand there," Jackson says. I resume position, sitting Indian-style on the floor. Jackson turns to Elliot. "Get it rolling, man. Do your thing."

"My…thing?"

"Loser. You're the ghost."

"Right." Elliot collects his duffel bag of goodies and walks to the back of the house.

"Spirits, if you're here, show yourselves," I say, palms facing up. There's shuffling, and then banging from above us.

"You hear that?" Jackson asks off screen.

There are two more thumps from above. I nod gravely, making sure my walkie is close enough for Elliot to hear what I'm saying. "Millie!" I call. "We wish you no harm. We only ask that you let your husband go about his day in peace. You're scaring him, Millie. If you can hear me, please. Show me you're with us."

We wait a moment. Two bumps come from the attic. A soft reply.

"Millie? Is that you?" I ask. More thumps from upstairs. I hear Elliot climb swiftly down the attic stairs. Beth keeps the camera off him, giving him time in the next room.

The lights flicker. I walk into the next room with our Infrared Camera. On the wall are dozens of handprints.

"That's impossible," I say, hamming it up. "Millie, you need to rest now. Let Mr. Hampton rest." I'm not sure how Elliot did it, but there are six or seven handprints on the ceiling, too.

Jackson nods to me from behind the camera, giving two thumbs up. Beth turns the camera off. "That was good," Jackson says.

"Where's Elliot?" I ask.

We find him dangling from an air vent.

"That's it?" he says. He holds a loose wooden board connected to a wire. "Found what was causing the banging," he says. "There are tons of loose boards up there. I secured a few. Probably should go up for all of them though."

"Good thinking," Jackson says. He tests a floorboard with his shoe. "We need to secure these, too," he says.

"You made a great ghost." I smile. Elliot gives me a small hug.

"Come on people," Jackson says. "Let's do this."

We go to work fixing the floorboards and make sure there are no loose beams. Then we replace rusty nails, tighten leaky faucets, wash the comforter on the bed, fluff the pillows, and even manage to lure two chipmunks out of the hole in the cupboard (with excessive amounts of cheese and whatever else we can find in Mr. Hampton's mostly empty fridge). By sunrise, the house is practically brand new, and if not that, at least it's tidier. Cleaner.

Still, I'm convinced Mr. Hampton isn't going to buy any of this. After all, we pretty much winged it, and none of us can really see ghosts. I keep practicing my poker face like Jackson taught me, expecting the worst, but when Mr. Hampton appears a little after dawn he takes in the house with fresh eyes.

"Did it work?" he says. "Is she resting? Our home…it looks different."

Jackson nods. "Of course. A successful 'cleansing' if I do say so myself. Here's the footage. We can watch it if you want. If you'd like to say goodbye."

If Mr. Hampton had any sense, he'd report us. I hold my breath as he reviews the images, thinking that there's no way in hell he'll fall for our low-rent scam. After the footage ends though, Mr. Hampton stares at the screen. It's a shoddy production. I know this, and Mr. Hampton should know this too, but when he doesn't say anything, Jackson smiles. "Why don't you rest up tonight? See if Millie comes back," he says.

Mr. Hampton nods absent-mindedly, and we show ourselves out.

Elliot shakes his head as we walk to the car. "That was weird," he says.

"It's like he forgot why we came," Beth replies.

"That's what we get when our clientele's pushing seventy," I say.

Jackson turns, surveying the house. "He'll come around."

The next morning though, Mr. Hampton doesn't come around, or call. He doesn't contact us that afternoon either. Jackson's sullen and quiet all day, waiting for the phone to ring. I can't help but be secretly glad, but I don't say anything. It's only later that night when I'm at the kitchen table watching Jackson cooking ramen noodles that I finally blurt out what I'm really thinking. "We gave it our best shot," I say. "Maybe we weren't meant to follow in Mom's footsteps."

Jackson eyes me over the steaming water. "Oh, ye of little faith," he says.

"I'm serious, Jackson. I mean, hey, it's probably for the best. That old man had no idea what we were doing. If anyone watched that footage they'd *know* we were liars."

"We'll get better," Jackson replies. "We'll adapt."

"Mr. Hampton's probably reporting us right now."

Jackson stirs his noodles. "Would you relax?" he says, but he's pensive, looking at the clock. At around six that night, Jackson says to hell with waiting and gives the old man a call. The gang looks on as the phone rings. Once. Twice. Three times. Then four. On the fifth ring Mr. Hampton picks up the phone.

"I don't know how you did it," Mr. Hampton says. "I've never slept this good in years."

"Tell all your friends," Jackson replies, high-fiving Elliot and then making arrangements to pick up the check.

After he hangs up the phone, Jackson slaps me on the

back. "You've done good," he says. "Really good. Now we just need to deal with this." He taps my head and winks.

I reassure myself that Mr. Hampton is our last client, and that surely no one will ever be foolish enough to call us again, but it doesn't happen like that. Word spreads fast. We refine our process. Jackson takes the lead even more than before, and the money starts flowing. We don't think much of it. We just keep going.

I get off the pills, like Jackson suggests. I'm not too happy about it, but Jackson insists there's no other way. "We need to work as a team," he says. "And those pills dull your senses." We're in the bathroom and he has my pill bottle poised over the toilet. With one nod, that's all it takes, he tips the plastic bottle and all those beautiful colored pills plop in the water. Flush. Even though I know there are ways to cheat Jackson, I want to make him proud too. Maybe there isn't anything to be scared of. Maybe the nightmares *are* all in my head.

More and more clients call. Our business grows. We even appear on the local news and get our photo snapped for the paper, though our smiling faces in the photo are unnaturally pale, making us appear ghoulish and out of place. The reporter asks us questions: "And what sort of training did you receive? Did your mother teach you everything you know?"

Jackson coaches everyone to sound vague, but motivational, so we don't really answer any questions at all, and surprisingly enough, his plan works. For some reason unforeseen to me, everyone just nods and smiles, accepting what we do, even calling it a whimsical part of the community. Townsfolk shake our hands. "Good job," they say, making our scheme seem almost okay, even harmless.

At night, I begin to dream about the faces of our clients, their hopeful, tortured eyes just wanting peace. It makes me toss and turn, thinking about how happy they are when the noises stop, and all it takes is a new nail in a floorboard, the removal of a dead raccoon in the wall, the organization of a basement's clutter, changing an old light bulb or straightening a step so it doesn't creak.

These ghosts, these stupid, stupid ghosts, are easily disposed of by merely cutting back the branches on a tree or providing a little landscaping in the backyard. Most of our clients just need someone to look after them, to make sure there are no loose ends.

Afterwards, without fail, we walk around the house with our clients like good old friends, clasping hands, sometimes exchanging hugs. None of them ever ask for a refund, though they do wonder where the ghosts go after we're done. Nowhere and everywhere, I want to say, because all the ghosts vanish once we leave the perimeters, disappearing into the ether. Like magic. Voilà.

2

I don't want to go to the house on Maple Drive, but Jackson says if I bail, everyone will know we're a sham. So, I go. I get in the car and we drive up into this polished neighborhood with perfect cars and perfect families. Except everything *isn't* perfect. That's the thing about death. It touches everyone. Even people with perfect lawns.

Elliot is checking all of the equipment beside me, while Jackson hums to the song on the radio, tapping his hands on the wheel. Even Beth is singing along. All I want to do is to crawl back into bed and not think about what we're doing, but Jackson will never go for that. Especially since I'm the main attraction.

The car chugs up the hill, stopping at a red light. Then the engine coughs. The starter catches, rolls, and then completely dies.

Jackson curses and cranks the ignition. Next to us, there's this polished lady in a SUV. She glances over at our dented

Chevy Tahoe and brushes back her hair with perfectly manicured nails.

"Should've taken it in," I say.

"Shut up, Ange," Jackson replies. He cranks it again. The engine whirs pathetically.

"You're gonna flood it," Elliot says. For just a second I entertain the possibility that he's standing up for me too.

"We'd already be there if *someone* wasn't late…" Jackson glances back at Elliot.

"I told you. Need to build my creds at the firm. Besides, I can't exactly put this on my resume."

"Why the hell not?" Jackson counters.

"I don't know. Some of us actually want to finish college?" Elliot replies.

"Guys, guys," Beth says, her voice strained. Jackson senses her annoyance and places his hand on her leg. Beth's real dream is to work for a big marketing firm in New York City. I think Jackson's charm is the only thing keeping her here.

"This is a sign," I say. "We should turn back."

"Oh, here we go." Jackson pats the car. "Don't listen to these haters. You got this, girl. Come on. Come *on*."

The light turns green, and the lady with the SUV drives off. We sit idly for a few more seconds. Jackson mutters under his breath, coaxing the car to start. And then, just like that, Jackson gets lucky. The starter catches. The engine turns over. Jackson smirks, throwing me a sideways glance.

The man that lives on Maple Drive is named Frank. We park on the street, not bothering with the driveway, and when Frank opens the door there are these dark circles under his eyes. He looks like a dressed down businessman with his crisp buttoned up shirt and sleeves rolled up. Although I don't mean to compare, I can't help thinking about my father and how I've never seen him wear anything remotely ironed.

Pattering footsteps echo down the hall. A little girl runs up and clings to Frank's leg.

"This is Carrie," Frank says, smiling sadly at his daughter. She looks to be about six. When Frank says her name, she stares up at us with wide eyes.

Jackson kneels down in front of her. "Nice to meet you, Carrie," he says. She hesitates and glances at her dad.

"Go ahead, baby doll," Frank says.

Carrie holds out her tiny hand to Jackson. He smiles warmly to her. "We're going to make everything all better. All right?"

My stomach flips as Carrie nods. Jackson stands and gestures to Elliot and Beth. We all help wheel a cart full of computer and video equipment inside the house. Frank holds the door open for us, his eyes lingering on me. I tell myself I just need to get through the next few hours. As long as I don't blow my cover, I don't let anyone down.

Jackson gathers the team, continuing with the pleasantries. "So, this is Beth, our computer wiz."

Beth gives Frank and Carrie a small wave.

"And Elliot. Sound and video technician. He also specializes in EMF readings. Helps point us in the right direction. You know, so we're not taking up too much of your time."

"How's it going?" Elliot smiles.

I have to admit, Jackson really could sell anything. He

is at once charming and modest, gauging how to make the customer feel at ease. My brother grabs my shoulders. "And this is my sister, Angela," he says, as if showing off a prize.

Frank's eyes flicker with hope. He holds out his hand. "Of course," he says. "The one with the gift. That report on the news. What you did for the Mulligans. Amazing."

I timidly shake his hand. "Here to help," I say.

The Mulligans had a severe rat infestation. Elliot installed some traps and we went hunting for them through the walls. It was a tricky case, but after a few days, the pitter-patter of little ghosts was gone. That would have been the end of it, but the Mulligans were so grateful they kept blabbing about our spirit catching skills to anyone that would listen. When the local news decided to do a story on us, the Mulligans were notorious around town. The news team made sure they were on the segment.

Beth clears her throat. "Where can we set up?" she asks.

"Oh. Um, let's see…" Frank says.

"Should be somewhere far enough from the 'activity.' We won't want to disturb what Ange's doing," Jackson says.

Frank nods and squeezes Carrie's shoulder. "Baby doll, how about you wash up for bed, okay?"

The basement is filled with dusty boxes and mannequins. They're neatly arranged and labeled, which is more than I can say for the other houses we've been in. Elliot stands on a stepladder. I pass him a small video camera that he rigs to the wall. His face scrunches in concentration.

This is how it goes. First we set up the job, everyone playing our parts, and then we get to work. It's rather simple, like clockwork now. We've come a long way from those first few gigs, though none of our progress makes me feel better about what we do.

Beth's voice crackles through Elliot's walkie. "Okay, try it now."

Elliot adjusts the setting on the video feed.

"Again," Beth says. They go back and forth like this. Turning knobs, calibrating dials. I head upstairs where Jackson and Beth have set up the equipment in the den. Beth's by the computers as Jackson keeps Frank busy, making sure to ask him lots of questions so he's *just* distracted enough that he can't fully pay attention to what we're doing. It's all in the details. That's what Jackson always says, and he's right.

When Jackson's done talking to Frank, it's my turn. Frank waits expectantly for me as he sits on a leather couch. His smile is warm, his eyes kind. I try to ignore all that.

"Do you happen to have any pictures of your wife?" I ask. "It helps with communicating." He nods and reaches over to a framed photo on a table. It's a family shot. The middle-aged woman in the photo is gaunt and bald from chemotherapy. She sits arm-in-arm with Frank and Carrie. Everyone's smiling like nothing's wrong, but their eyes are troubled.

I take notes in a journal, jotting down little tidbits, as Frank talks: *Her name was Madeline. She liked apricots and Bolognese. She had this high-pitched, beautiful laugh. She'd read three books to Carrie every night. Her favorite color was green.*

When there's a lull in Frank's speech, I clear my throat. "Madeline. Is that what you called her? Or what her friends called her? Did she have any pet names? Nicknames?"

"Maddy. Everyone called her Maddy."

Elliot moves through the room waving an EMF meter, pushing it near the walls.

"What's that? What's he doing?" Frank asks.

"Oh. Checking electromagnetic fields." I try to sound as confident as Jackson, but my voice seems high-pitched and strange.

Frank studies Elliot. "Is it...are you getting anything?"

"Definitely," Elliot says. "Especially in the basement. Really hot down there."

Frank nods, clenching and unclenching his hands. "She used to run a tailoring business out of the basement. Spent a lot of time there. We didn't need the money. She just really enjoyed it. Creating."

Frank's cheek trembles. I pretend to write something down. *Please don't cry*, I think. *Please don't lose it.* It's harder when they cry. Harder to fake that I have the answers.

"It's been touch and go," Frank says. "Especially with Carrie. She's so young. One step forward, couple steps back. You know?"

"Yeah," I say, a familiar ache echoing in my ribcage.

"How long ago was it for you?" Frank studies me. "With your mother?"

I smile, trying to keep my voice steady. "Ten years. This December."

"I read the article on your website." Frank pats my hand reassuringly. "Must've been difficult."

"It's okay. Thanks." I silently curse Jackson. I told him to take down that article, though I know why he keeps it up. People love hearing about how tragic it is that our mother offed herself. It makes me sick, and I almost want to get up and run to the bathroom, but I hold my ground. The sooner we do this, the sooner we can go home.

Frank continues talking about Maddy. He tells me they'd get in fights sometimes, but would always manage to make up in a couple of hours. I smile when Frank tells me this, but mostly I try to not hold on too tightly to what he says. It's haunting enough remembering the fragments of strangers we've worked with in the past.

We should have started by now, but Jackson is nowhere to be found. I excuse myself from Frank and go looking for my brother. Down the hall, a little past the kitchen, the toilet flushes. I hear rummaging and the faucet turning on and off. The door opens abruptly and Jackson rolls out, his eyes red. When he sees me, his sniffs hard.

"Why are you standing there? Let's do this." He wipes his nose. Sometimes Jackson needs a little help to get through the day. It's not coke, what he snorts. It's something else with a long name that I can't pronounce. You'd think he'd grow out of it by now, especially with his quest to keep me off my crazy pills, but I guess even he needs a little pick-me-up. Still, Beth wouldn't be happy if she caught him like this.

I follow Jackson back to the others. When Frank goes to check on Carrie, Jackson quietly debriefs us. My stomach churns.

"Take your time," Jackson says to me. "Remember, you need to be thorough."

"Got it," I say, my voice clipped.

"Any trouble, we're right here. What's wrong?" Jackson asks. "You look like shit."

"Nothing," I say. "I'm just not feeling well."

He frowns. The floorboards creak above our heads. "Buck up, sis. We need this one."

Frank moves down the stairs. Jackson walks over to greet him, his game face on.

I head down the hallway, Elliot close behind me. This whole day feels off, like I'm walking through quicksand. I'll find myself staring off into space, and then my whole body will feel buoyant, as if I'm floating away. It doesn't make any sense, and I know the others wouldn't understand, though Elliot would probably listen more than my brother or Beth.

Elliot turns the camera on when I reach the basement. The door creaks as I open it wide. Only a faint amount of light leads down the uneven stairs. I click on the flashlight we've brought with us. I've seen my fair share of basements in the last year. Even though I should be used to them by now, it still seems like I'm descending into the pit of hell with every new house we enter. I think about how everyone is gathered by the computer monitors in the den, watching my every move. *Don't mess this up, Ange*, I think. *Everyone's counting on you.*

I'm about to take the first step when Carrie peers around the corner. She's dressed in her pajamas and lets out a whine. "Daddy? What's happening?"

Frank appears behind her. He whispers 'sorry' to us. "It's okay, sweetie. Go back to bed." He picks Carrie up and she rests her chin on his shoulder. They slip back into the den.

"You ready?" Elliot asks.

The steps look rickety and small. My hands shake. As soon as this is over, I'll never have to see Frank and his adorable daughter again. What's the big deal? Why do I care? *Because you have a conscience.* I clench and unclench my fists.

"Want to take a minute?" Elliot asks.

"No. I'll be alright."

Slowly, I take one step, and then another. People's basements are all different, but there's a heaviness to them that unnerves me. Sometimes it seems like I can feel the memories of objects, and in rooms with so many forgotten *things*, it can be tiring. Not to mention I'm pretty sure I'm afraid of the dark, though I'd never admit this to Jackson. He made fun of me enough as a kid when I'd wake up screaming in the night.

As my feet touch the cool cement basement floor, I scan the space, waiting for my eyes to adjust to the dark. Even though the basement is as we've left it, the boxes neatly stacked around us, I feel tilted, as if I'm seeing everything for the first time.

My eyes rest on three mannequins draped in fabric, the makings of unfinished dresses hang from their limbs. I remind myself that Maddy was a seamstress and this is just the remains of her past life.

"Maddy? We're here to help. Okay?" I say. "You don't have to be afraid."

We move deeper into the basement, past the boxes and shelves. In the middle of the room, a faint ringing noise drifts into my ears. I touch my head.

"My name is Angela Sayers. Your husband, Frank, called me here," I say, struggling to stay focused. "I'm here to ask you…if you would consider leaving this house."

A wave of nausea hits me. I've done this so many times

before, why is today any different? Sleep. I need sleep. With a deep breath, I hold my ground, waiting for Beth's signal. Jackson's gone over the routine in detail, covering all the bases. What happens now is he gives Beth the signal by the computers, tapping her on the shoulder, or maybe touching her wrist with his hand. Then she'll discretely brush one of the keys and the waveform monitor will blip.

The voices are already programmed into the system. Sometimes it's a whisper, other times it's a hiss or a giggle. It gets the client every time. But I try not to think about that now, Frank with his desperate face, so hopeful to connect with his lost love.

I hear the click on my walkie. Once. Twice. The signal. There it is. Maybe after this I can sleep. Sleep is nice. Dreaming not so much, but sleep, the act of closing my eyes, of not being *here*.

"Your husband," I say to the shadows. "Your daughter. They love you. But they need to move on."

The ringing in my ears grows louder. Sharper. Piercing. What the…? My head throbs. "Carrie misses you. Very much. But she needs to grow up happy. Normal."

I steady myself, the words hitting a little too close to home. Having a mother as a medium doesn't exactly constitute a normal childhood.

"Do we have an understanding?" When there's silence, I take another step, delving deeper into the basement. The programmed whispers should be coming through by now.

"Maddy? Do we have an understanding…?"

Suddenly, my legs feel hollow. Something in the air has shifted. I'm not sure what it is. My eyes widen, trying to take in what little light there is. What is it? What's changed? I survey the misshapen lumps around me, and that's when I notice there's something different about the room. The boxes are all where they're supposed to be, so are the shelves, the mannequins…

Wait. The mannequins. I count the bodies. A chill runs up my spine. There's a fourth mannequin. But this one's not draped in fabric. It's just a dark human shape. Even from here I can see that it's gaunt and bald. Madeline?

Get a grip, Ange. Hold it together.

I shake my head, trying to come to terms with the image. The face is unreadable in the shadows, but it's looking my way. *She's* looking my way. I feel my heartbeat quicken. I'm not sure what to do. I know they're watching me upstairs, I can't just run. What would they say? Elliot is still behind me. He adjusts some settings on the camera, not aware that I'm hyperventilating in front of him. When he sees me eyeing him, he winks.

The ringing grows louder. Drifting in and out like a storm siren. I take a step back, clutching my head. Elliot lowers the camera a little.

"Ange, you okay?" he asks.

The figure continues to sway. It's sickly and hunched over. My arms tremble. I push them against my sides. "You see her, right? Do you?"

Elliot's eyes widen. "See who?"

My eyes water. The cold, drafty air rips from my lungs. The ringing taunts me as the figure leans forward, swaying. *I'm okay*, I think. *I'm okay.* And for a second, I believe it.

That is until the mannequin bolts toward me.

My voice erupts as the mannequin, Maddy, whatever, reaches out a pale, lanky arm, veins like coiling snakes cutting through her skin. I let out a blood-curdling scream. Crab-walking backwards, my face hot and flushed, I trip over a pair of boxes.

Elliot tries to hold me, but I turn away. "Ange, it's me," he says. "It's just me." He grabs my shoulders and I jump. "You saw that, right? You saw her?" I ask.

When Elliot finally gets me to calm down, I look around the basement, breathing deeply. The pale figure is gone. There's no one else here. It's just Elliot and me. For some reason an image of my mother flashes through my mind, how tired she looked all the time. She was always talking about people that weren't there. Dread courses through me. *I am not her,* I think. *I am not crazy.*

Elliot rubs my back. He cups my face between my hands. It's a sudden intimate gesture, and it brings me back to reality. He smiles. "Let's get the hell out of here," he says.

3

Jackson lets out a yowl as he clinks glasses with me and the gang. We're seated at a plush booth in the only nightclub in town. It's so dark I can't even make out the cigarette stains on the pleather couch. We knock back our shots, and I cringe as the bitter liquid slides down my throat.

"One more! One more!" Jackson says. He refills from a private bottle, sputtering and laughing, and holds his shot in the air.

"Hey. Okay. This one's to us. We really got it down to a science. Beth, perfectly on cue with the voices. Elliot, your recon was spot-on. I thought that guy was going to *weep* when you mentioned the basement."

Elliot does a little bow, ever humble.

Then, surprisingly, Jackson turns to me. "And to little sis. Normally, you phone it in, but tonight? That was a *pimp* Oscar performance. To us!"

I manage a small smile, still thinking about the bolting

mannequin. I'm not sure how they did it. All I can reason is that Jackson and Elliot rigged the mannequin on some sort of pulley system when I wasn't around. Whatever it is, it's a new tactic, and I'm not a fan.

We all toss back the shots. Jackson pounds the table excitedly. "See?! And you guys wanted to get *real* jobs. How else are you going to make this kind of money in one night?"

Jackson pulls Beth closer. She resists at first, but then places her hand on his chest. Even from here, I can tell Jackson's mind is whirring a mile a minute. He talks in circles and then hits the side of the couch with his fist. "Shit. I forgot. Babe, show El."

"What?" Beth asks.

"The new site. Pull it up," Jackson says.

Beth rummages around in her purse as Jackson nudges her. "Hang on, hang on," she says. "Here." She hands her phone to Elliot.

"She even put up the Good Morning America clip where Mom faints. Sick, right?" Jackson says.

A tingly heat creeps up my neck. Elliot scrolls through the website. *Sayers Medium Service* is in bright, bold letters at the top of the page. I've probably told Jackson thirty times I didn't want anything related to our mother on the website. I lean over Elliot's shoulder and see numerous rows of YouTube videos of her in psychic garb. Instead of yelling at Jackson, I focus on digging my fingernails in my forearm.

Elliot reads over the website. "I thought we were losing the articles."

Jackson waves his hand as if shooing a fly. "Why?

Because Ange wanted to?" He turns his attention to Beth. End of discussion.

Elliot glances in my direction. He hands the phone back to Jackson. "Cool," he says dismissively. Jackson just grins.

I grab the vodka and refill my shot glass. With one quick motion, I tilt my head back and down the liquor. Then I fill the shot glass again.

"There you go, sis!" Jackson cheers.

I can feel Elliot's gaze as I swallow the harsh liquid. The burn is slow and sweet. No wonder my father likes this stuff. Forcing a smile, I grab Elliot's hand.

"Come on. Let's dance!" I say, pulling him away from the table.

The dance floor is already packed with sweating bodies. It's hard to breathe as we sway under the swirling lights. The bass reverberates under my skin. Elliot leans in, whispering in my ear. I feel his hot breath on my neck, but when I look up I stare into the face of someone I've never met. Scanning the crowd, I see Elliot's not even close to me, but at the bar. How did that happen? He's talking to a girl with long eyelashes who smiles at whatever he says.

A wave of jealousy swells within me, but I push it down, closing my eyes. My sweaty hair sticks to my face. For just a moment, as the bloops and blips take over, I've lost myself. I'm just another body dancing in the dark, bumping up against strangers. I let the pain of what I can't have wash away.

And it feels great. I'm just like everyone else, dancing, laughing. Jackson howls to the DJ, suddenly beside me. He jumps up and down. I let out a little yelp and raise my arms to the flickering lights.

My hazy eyes drift around, searching through the tangle of arms and legs. The room spins. People laugh and flirt. I rock my head to the music. Through the crowd, halfway to the bar, a small shadow crouches by itself. Not moving.

Straining to see amidst the bouncing lights, I make out that it's a man wearing gold chains around his neck. He's looking straight at me, but something's wrong with his arms. I squint, studying the man. His arms are misshapen, his shirt dangling in wisps from his shoulders. And that's when I realize…this man has no arms. He falls to the floor. Amidst the strobe lights I see he only has stubs for legs, too. I step back, into Elliot, who's by my side once again. He laughs and hugs me.

Time speeds up, and then it slows down, but all I hear is ringing. Low and dull. The man, that *thing* with the gold chains, comes towards me. He's only half a person. No one else seems to notice that he's here, crawling among us.

The lights illuminate the man. He opens his garish mouth. A section of his torso is missing, as if he's been ripped apart. Glistening blue intestines hang from his side like tangled rope.

I'm drunk. That's all. This isn't real. But then why do his beady eyes look so desperate? They fixate on me as he struggles to come closer, his face wrenched in agony.

I scream, pushing back again, this time spilling my drink on a Bro with this devastatingly strong cologne. The Bro whirls around. "Hey, what's your problem?"

The Bro sneers, but I'm still looking behind me, checking people's feet for the thing coming towards me. All around us people grope and thump and pulse and pound. But the man with the gold chains is gone.

Bro Cologne looks at me like I've flown the coop, and hell, maybe I have. Deep pressure erupts from my chest. I hiccup. "Nice perfume," I say. "What is that? Eau de fuck you?"

Bro Cologne narrows his eyes. He looks behind me, to Elliot. "Why don't you control your girl?" he says. As my face reddens, Elliot stands there, his mouth open as if he's not processing what Bro Cologne said.

"Excuse me?" I say. "Excuse *me*?" I get in Bro Cologne's face. His breath reeks of vodka. Elliot steps beside me, placing a sweaty hand on my shoulder.

"You heard me. Crazy," Bro Cologne says, and it's *that* word, the word Jackson and my father call my mother, and the way he says it, so dismissively, as if that sums up my entire existence.

I don't mean to do it. I don't even think. I hack up a wad of spit and catapult it into his face. Elliot steps in, grabbing my arm lightly. "I…Ange. Hey, come on."

I expect Bro Cologne to charge, but he just stares me down. Maybe he really does see the crazy in my eyes.

"Good luck with that, man," he says to Elliot, and his tone is just so pitying it makes me even angrier.

I squirm away from Elliot's grasp. "Did Mommy stone wash those jeans for you or did you pay $300 for somebody else to do it?"

"Shut your mouth." A skinny girl dances nearby and Bro Cologne pulls her closer. *Even this guy has someone.* He sees me watching and sneers. "Bitch," he says.

And with that, I kick him hard in the junk. So hard his body folds and a whooshing sound escapes his lips.

Club goers gawk as other Frat guys rush to the aid of their fallen brother.

"Jesus," Elliot says. "Time to go. *Ange*." He yanks my arm, dragging me the hell out of there.

• • •

Jackson swerves into the dirt driveway. He's talking a mile a minute. Beth can't keep her hands off him. I rest my head on the car seat, my mind drifting back to that misshapen shadow on the dance floor. Was it just my imagination? If it was, why did it feel so real?

Jackson roars with laughter. "Bro cologne! Genius," he says.

He stretches his fist towards me and doesn't move until I half-heartedly fist bump him. Stumbling out of the car, he kisses Beth as they grope each other under the pale moonlight. I think of Elliot and how I want him to touch me that way. A warm blush creeps up my neck.

Elliot's being unnaturally quiet next to me. After we watch Jackson and Beth fondle each other for a few more moments, he jumps out of the car.

"I'm going to take off," he says. "Got an early class tomorrow."

Jackson points Elliot's way. "Aw, hike your skirt up, Sally."

"I'll catch up with you tomorrow."

Jackson's too focused on Beth to respond. She laughs as Jackson grabs her. We watch them stagger back to the house.

There's a slight pause. "Taking this engineering thing seriously, aren't you?" I say.

Elliot shrugs. "Seem to be pretty good at it. And I figured I might as well have an honest job after all this. Help my folks out."

"That's nice," I say.

"Yeah. Nice." Elliot kicks the ground with his shoe. "They frustrate the hell out of me, though. They're all right wing this, small government that. Meanwhile, they're living on food stamps. But whatever. It's family." He laughs, and even though I'm not exactly sure what he said, I laugh too. Our eyes lock.

"Sure you don't want to hang?" I ask. "Late night pizza?" I brush his hand. He grabs my finger. We stand there for a few seconds. A mess of emotions bubbles inside me. I've known Elliot for years, but I can't tell what he's thinking. He searches my face.

"Earlier tonight," he says. "In the basement. You seemed…pretty freaked out."

"Yeah," I say. "I just wasn't expecting it. At first I thought I was going insane, but then I figured it had to be Jackson. Of course." Anger surges through me. "I could kill him. I know it's more authentic having me be surprised, but I could've used a warning when she attacked."

Elliot knits his brow. "When who attacked?"

"You guys had to have snuck in before or something. It was a pulley system, wasn't it? What else could make it move?"

Elliot stares at me. "Ange, I've known you half my life, and it's true Jackson can be a jerk. But I have no idea what you're talking about."

I take in his concerned gaze and how his hand squeezes

mine. Slowly, I pull back, my mind racing, and fiddle with the buttons of my jacket. "Forget it," I say, forcing a smile. Elliot shuffles from foot to foot, our magic moment deflated.

"Anyway," Elliot says. "I'll see you, okay?"

He heads to his car and hops in. The tires squeal as the car peels off. I look up just in time to see his taillights vanish in the night.

•   •   •

I sit on my bed inspecting the *no refills* tab printed on my empty prescription bottle. Maybe Jackson's wrong. Maybe I do need these pills, even if it's all in my head. Maybe I'm not as strong as him. Though Jackson's one to talk, he can't go a night without some sort of fix.

The room seems to bend around me. I brush my fingers over the fine print of the prescription bottle. With my head still pounding from the vodka shots, I open my laptop and click to a web browser. But what am I looking for?

I type in 'going insane' but that just depresses me, so I delete the search. Next up, I take my time spelling out the word doctors used to describe my mother: s-c-h-i-z-o-p-h-r-e-n-i-c.

As articles pop up, I scroll through and picture my mother in the psych ward, her hands over her ears. She had pulled out most of her hair by then, and her eyes were always darting, searching for people that weren't there.

A flood of chat forums unfurl on screen. Clicking through them, I scan the headlines, but there's nothing useful. Leaning forward, I keep reading.

On the other side of the wall, Jackson's bed begins to squeak, the bedsprings bouncing rhythmically. Beth cries out.

I cover my ears, but I still hear my brother grunt. Even the lamp shakes on the nightstand.

"Seriously?" I say.

The moans become louder, harder, faster. I push a pillow over my head, trying to drown out the noise. When that doesn't work, I grab my laptop and seek refuge on the porch.

On the worn couch by the pot of wilted herbs, I huddle under a ratty quilt as my breath vaporizes in front of me. Past the crooked trees, the sun slowly rises. I watch the sky turn pink and red until I can't keep my eyes open anymore.

· · ·

Ring-Ring. Ring-Ring.

Deep-seated pressure pounds against my skull. Lifting my head, I rub my face. I'm curled up in the fetal position, and although my hands are numb, it's the first time I've slept in days.

Ring-Ring.

Disentangling myself from the blanket, I stumble inside. "Jackson? Beth?" I check the clock on the stove. It's about noon. The phone rings again. "Okay, okay," I mutter. Each shrill ring makes my head pound more. I pick up the phone.

"Hello?" Static. "Hello?"

"Yes?" The frail voice of an elderly woman crackles through the line. "Is this the Medium Service?"

"It is," I reply.

There's silence on the other end, then a sigh of relief. "Thank heavens. I'm looking at your website here. Can you help me?"

I shift from foot to foot. "What's the nature of your problem?"

"Oh." The elderly woman's voice catches. She clears her throat. "It's the children," she says. "I can't get them to stop screaming."

I press the phone into my ear, wondering if I've heard her correctly. "Children? Look, if this is some prank…"

"Please don't hang up. They've been so loud, you see. I haven't slept."

"They?" I ask.

The elderly woman's voice trembles. "The girls. I hear them. Every night. Since the accident it's been worse."

Even though I know Jackson would kill me, I consider hanging up the phone. "Where are you located?" I ask.

"Down near Wakefield," the elderly lady continues. "Off Highway 31. Cypress Street. Number 624. My name's Mrs. Green. I used to run a foster home."

A knot coils in my stomach. Why does that sound familiar? *Something happened there. Something bad.*

"Hello? Please. How soon can you come out?"

"Um…well." I tap my fingers against the receiver. "We're, uh, busy right now, so…I don't think we…"

"Please. I'll pay you twice your fee."

"Sorry, we're…I'm sorry."

I fumble with the phone. *Hang up*, I think. *Hang up.*

And with a deep breath, I do.

Click.

I stare at the phone, thinking about how I could use some Tylenol, but I don't move to the kitchen. I don't move. Instead, I contemplate that address, 624 Cypress, and how

I can't remember what happened there, though I know it wasn't good.

Ring-Ring. Ring-Ring.

I jump back, startling myself. The phone rings again. I turn and grab my laptop, heading up the stairs to my room, but even with my bedroom door closed, I can still hear Jackson's measured voice on the answering machine: "You've reached the Sayers Medium Service…"

On my bed, I search for '624 Cypress James County'. Various headlines unfurl:

THIRD GIRL GOES MISSING
POLICE HAVE NO LEADS
SIX GIRLS MISSING
SON, HERMAN GREEN, INVESTIGATED
FOSTER HOME SHUT DOWN
HERMAN GREEN FLEES, NO TRACE
SKELETAL REMAINS FOUND

It keeps going. Article after article. The words are bad enough, but the images…black and white photos of the girls' gleeful faces, coupled with the grim expressions of policemen, and then there's Herman Green himself, a twenty-something boy with a blank face and broad shoulders. A slight smile dances across his lips. He looks kind, even handsome, which disturbs me even more. Was the photo taken before he committed the crimes?

Reaching for my bedroom drawer, I pop two Advil and then slam the laptop shut. From downstairs, the phone rings again. Mrs. Green's desperate voice warbles on the answering machine. "Hello?" she says. "Please. Is anybody there?" I listen as Mrs. Green breathes on the phone. "Hello?" She sighs audibly and then hangs up.

I creep down the stairs. The house is silent now. Outside, Jackson's car pulls up in the driveway. A red light blinks on the answering machine. It chirps with a new message. Beth's laughter rises from the yard. Car doors slam.

Chirp.

My finger hovers over the erase button. If only it was that easy, one button and all your problems disappear.

Chirp.

I press my finger down. *Delete.*

4

I try not to look too bored as I sit in the corner with this forty-year-old dude named Sam. Sam's balding but hides it well with a semi-shaved head and a trim beard. Everything about this coffee shop is sterile and safe, with rules about how to wipe down the counters, how to take someone's money, how to make delicious drinks.

There's safety in knowing everything is in its place, and Sam looks like he's quite comfortable being the king of this world of fifteen minute breaks and friendly reminders to always greet customers when they walk through the door.

Sam grins warmly at me across the table, and I can tell he's well practiced in the art of smiling. "And, you're a student at VCU?"

"Was. I'm in a transitional phase. Also, kind of ran out of money. That's why I'm…you know."

"Sure, sure. What were you studying?"

"Psych. Yeah." I pick underneath my fingernails. When

I catch him looking, I sit on my hands. Dappled light shines through the big floor to ceiling windows. At this point it's not even about the money, it's about doing something that doesn't involve Jackson and his quest to tell me how to live my life. If I can't escape myself, then I can at least try to escape him.

"Always found that fascinating. Human brain. Cool stuff."

"Yep," I say, sharing an awkward smile with Sam. Is he flirting with me? He keeps holding my gaze a little too long. I'm not sure whether to stare back or look down. Working at a coffee shop for nine dollars an hour is not my ideal scenario, but it's all I can think of on such short notice.

"Anyway, sorry." Sam smiles. "They make me ask everyone this. 'Why do you want to be a part of the Starbucks family?'"

I can't help but snicker. Sam does too.

"I know," he says. "Cheesy, right?"

"It's fine. You want me to answer?"

He chuckles again, but it's a little strained. "Need to write something here, so…"

"Um, well. I'm friendly," I say. A sharp pain shoots through my temples. "I love coffee…" My right ear goes silent, and then a faint ringing echoes through that ear. I wince.

Not now, I think. *Please, not here.* I try to keep smiling. The ringing moves to my left ear. It's low and steady. "I…I've always gotten along with everyone. Except my brother." Forcing a nervous laugh, I try to concentrate as the ringing grows. *Stay calm,* I think. *Stay calm.*

In the distance, over Sam's shoulder, I notice a businessman in a faded suit. He limps towards us from the other side of the glass window. Pressure builds behind my eyes. The businessman looks like he's walking through quicksand. I brush my hands over my face, forcing myself to focus. "I… work well in…"

Each step the businessman takes causes the ringing in my head to grow louder. I'm still talking to Sam, but I can't hear my own voice. My throat constricts, the ringing taking over. Sam appears to be following along, but there's now a puzzled expression on his face. *Can't breathe. Can't breathe.*

The businessman halts behind Sam. Slowly, he peers into the window. His face is gaunt. Mouth agape. When his bloodshot eyes find mind, bile rises in my throat. I am officially going crazy. Either that or this man is officially dead. Both scenarios are not good.

Sam must agree with me, because he suddenly stops smiling. His eyes widen. "Um," he says, motioning to my nose. "You've got a…"

I feel a soft dribble below my nostril and bring a hand to my face. A streak of blood smears my fingers.

"Excuse me," I say.

Stumbling outside, I rush over to a trashcan and retch, again and again. After awhile, I'm just dry heaving. I glance in the window, and by the way Sam stares blankly back at me I know the interview is over. Trembling, I grasp the side of the trashcans. What the hell is happening to me?

• • •

Later that night, I walk into the kitchen to find Beth chasing Jackson around the counter. He's multi-tasking as he goes, filling a baggy with ice and pressing it to his face.

"Let me see it," she says.

"Don't touch me," Jackson replies.

"What'd he do to you?!" Beth says. "Show me. What'd he do?"

"Nothing. I'll deal with it."

"Jackson. *Let me see*."

He sighs and pulls the ice away. Not only does he have a split lip, there's a long gash across his forehead. I've seen Jackson get beat up like this before, and it's always from Nate, the sketchy dealer he buys pills from. You'd think he would've learned by now, but he just seems to be buying more and more, even when he's telling me to be strong.

Beth doesn't say anything when she gets a good look at him. She just shakes her head and storms up the stairs. When Jackson goes after her, I crawl onto the living room couch and flip on the TV. There has to be something I can do which doesn't involve scamming sad people out of money, but a girl with only two years of college doesn't really have a lot of choices. Flipping burgers? Waitressing? Retail?

I cover my face with the blanket and close my eyes, hoping that sleep will help. The phone rings in the next room. I don't answer it. Footsteps stomp down the stairs. A few seconds later I hear Jackson's voice: "Sayers Medium Service." He listens. "Yeah. No, we're available. Who told you that?"

Shit. I walk to the doorway and peer into the kitchen, watching Jackson's face knot in frustration. Something *thunks* upstairs. There's banging. Loud claps. "What're you doing?" Jackson shouts up the stairs. He hangs up the phone and eyes me. "I want to talk to you," he says.

Behind him, Beth lugs her suitcase down the steps, her jacket and purse under one arm. "I'm going," Beth says.

"Going?" Jackson says. There's panic in his voice. "*Where?*"

"New York. With or without you. I told you I'm done with this."

"He'll follow me. He's got people there." Jackson goes to Beth, but she pulls away, her lips drawn in a thin, red line.

"Without you then," she says, opening the door.

He grabs the suitcase from her, trying to calm her down. It's hard to see my brother this way. I know how much Beth means to him.

"Wait. Hey. One more gig, alright?" Jackson says.

Beth sighs. "I'm through, Jackson. I can't stay here. It isn't a life."

"That was a really big call just now. Gonna pay us double our quote."

Beth perks up a little, but my stomach flips. He cups Beth's face in his hands. "I swear," he says. "I pay off Nate, and then we're gone. You and me. I can't be without you. Please."

I back away, wanting to get the hell out of there, but when I'm almost out of sight Jackson looks up. "What'd you say to that old lady?" he asks.

"Old lady?" Beth asks.

The skin around Jackson's eye is turning purple. "Jackson, seriously. You should keep ice on that," I say.

"She just called. Said you turned her down."

I meet my brother's gaze, trying to keep a straight face, but I've never been a good liar. "I'm just tired of it," I say. "Like Beth said, I'm through. Each time I do a gig, the nightmares get worse. We don't have the equipment to cover a place that big anyway."

"We'll fake it. Lady sounds ancient. She won't know the difference."

"Scary shit has happened in that house, Jackson."

He groans. "Like thirty years ago."

"Are you listening to yourself?"

He picks at the cut on his arm. "Come on. It's going to be like every other gig. 'Oh my dead kid, I miss her. My dead wife, she won't leave us alone. Boo hoo.' We're going to get in. We're going to get out. We're going to make some money. And as for those nightmares you're having? I can't believe we're still discussing those."

"You always say that, but…"

"This lady needs us, Ange. It's as simple as that. You think she wants the truth? That she wants to hear the voices that haunt her are just in her head? All we have to do is show up, put on a damn good show, and she sleeps better at night."

"That has nothing to do with…"

"The woman wants to pay double our rate so that she can move on, and you want to deny her that? It's a no-brainer. We all need the money."

"I don't know, Jackson. How much does that shit you're snortin' cost these days?"

A flash of anger crosses Jackson's face. "You really want to go there?" He steps closer. "Ever since Mom offed herself, all you've done is judge me. About how I dealt with it, or didn't deal with it. But you're the one that can't hold a job…"

"Okay," Beth says. "Maybe let's not do this now." She

tries to get in-between us, but Jackson points a finger in my face.

"You're the one who carries this shit around with you all day. You're the one that freaks out at the thought of any guy touching you. Oh, unless it happens to be your brother's childhood best friend, right? Cause, yeah. He's really going to go for you."

"Jackson, come on," Beth says.

Tears brim in my eyes, but I don't want to show that he's getting to me.

"Face it, sis," Jackson says. "You can run away to dead end jobs and dull your mind with those pills, but you're still going to be a freak. Doing this…it's the only thing you'll ever be good at. Making people believe you're a nut bag. Cause you know what? It ain't much of a stretch!"

I look my brother dead in the eyes. My chin trembles. "Go to hell," I say. He laughs. It's the worst way to respond. Whirling around, I head for the door.

Jackson calls after me, "Fine. We're doing it without you then! Have fun pouring coffee, or whatever!"

• • •

I've been pushing trusty Green Bean for hours, straining my old station wagon harder than it needs to go. Even now the engine's groaning, but I'm almost there. Despite the peaceful farms and the lazy cows chewing grass in the fields, I can't help but smoke cigarette after cigarette. A few hundred feet away, I see a worn sign: *Norfolk. Next exit.* Turning the wheel, I make a quick right off the highway.

I'm always surprised how nothing really changes on my

street. The abandoned cars are still rusting by the weeds in our neighbor's yard. The white fence is still rotting around our house. I pull into the driveway of my childhood home, an old, two-story bungalow. Sitting in the driver's seat, I smoke my last cigarette and study the paint-chipped front porch, slowly building up the courage to get out of the car.

It's not that I don't like my father, or even that we don't get along, but going home always makes me think of my mother. She took her last breath in this house, and I don't like being reminded that she's no longer with us.

Walking steadily, I follow the cracked concrete steps up to the front door and knock. At first there's silence on the other side. I wonder if my father's sleeping, but then I hear lumbering footsteps.

"Who is it?" my father asks.

"It's me," I reply.

The door unlocks, whining open on old hinges. On the other side, my father blinks at me. His beer gut has grown since the last time I saw him and his t-shirt is stained, probably with motor oil or whatever he ate for dinner. I can already tell by how his eyes are bloodshot that he's been drinking. It takes a moment for him to recognize me.

"Christ," he says, opening the door wider.

At the kitchen table, my father fills two mugs of coffee and splashes some bourbon in his. He offers some to me, but I shake my head. There are unwashed dishes in the sink. The dishtowel is caked with crusty food. He sits down in the chair beside me, his knees creaking. "Believe me," he says. "I'd help if I could. But they finally caught onto my little disability racket. Checks stopped shown' up last month."

The lines on my father's face are worn. He's been drinking more and more since my mother's death. I look down, studying an ant trespassing across the kitchen table. "I'm surprised to see you," he says. "Usually it's your brother showin' up here, looking' for a handout. Half the time he looks so strung out I…Goddamn waste. He was always so smart."

"I'm not here for money," I reply.

"Oh," he says. My father tries to focus on my face. "How's school?" he says. "You still taking care of yourself?"

I shake my head. "I stopped going to classes. And no, I'm not taking the pills."

"Why'd the hell you do *that*?" His voice booms in the messy kitchen.

"I don't know. Maybe I didn't have the best role models growing up?" I sit back. "Look, I don't want to get into it. I just came to ask a question." I meet his gaze. "About Mom."

My father blinks. He puts his mug of coffee and bourbon down.

I follow my father up the rickety stairs and down the hall. We both don't like talking about my mother, and I feel like her spirit lingers in each and every corner of this house, which doesn't make being here any easier.

In his bedroom, my father bends down and rummages through an old dresser, digging out a dented coffee can from a drawer full of socks. He pops open the cap, revealing a wad of bills. There's maybe a couple fives and some crinkled ones.

"All I got left for the month. I want you to have it."

I shake my head, but he grabs my hand and folds the money in my palm.

"You need to handle this." His voice strains as he looks at me.

"I'm not taking the last of your cash."

"Goddamn it, Ange."

I place the money on the dresser. "I'll figure something out."

My father nods, though his eyes still search mine. On the shelf by the bed there's a photo of my mother sitting on a grassy campus lawn. She's smiling, and her teeth are a brilliant white.

"When did she…? How did it start for her? When did you know…something was wrong?" I ask.

My father gets this far away look in his eyes as he tries to remember. "She was getting these dizzy spells. Headaches. Said she was…seeing people. People that weren't there. Sometimes she'd get these nose bleeds…"

I must look alarmed, because my father squeezes my arm. "That ain't going to happen to you, though. We're going to figure this out."

Nodding, I look back to the photo. "Mind if I have this?" I ask.

Jackson and Beth are asleep when I slink through the front door. The wind groans against the shuttered windows. In my room, I set the photo down on my desk and flop onto my bed, studying my mother's face. Curling into a ball, I try not to panic. Outside, a dog barks. I curl up tighter, trying to drown out any other noises. Images rush behind my eyes. Shadows. Strangers. They dart in the corners of my mind, even though I try to shut them out.

I'm breathing heavy. My skin itches. It's cold, so cold. But maybe sleep will help. Maybe I won't dream…

I snap awake. Sitting up, I breathe deeply. Did I fall asleep? There's a tightness in my throat, like something's caught below my windpipe. I inhale and exhale, trying to get my bearings.

A faint whimper echoes down the hall. I slip out of bed, listening. After a moment, I walk cautiously down the hallway, the silence thick around me. Every now and then I'll hear that whimper and have to swallow the lump in my throat.

"Beth?"

Walking closer, I see the bathroom light is on. Jackson's bedroom door is open, but when I peek in the room, Jackson and Beth are sleeping, the sheets tangled between them. If they're here, then who's in the bathroom?

I take a deep breath, walking towards the closed bathroom door. Slowly, I reach out a trembling hand. Easing the door open, my eyes widen. A strange woman in a ratty blue nightgown is by the sink. Her back's to me, and she quakes violently, her shoulders shaking.

"It's too much…too much," she says, the blood pooling and dripping off the counter. Her red fingers stain the porcelain. On her right hand she wears a simple wedding ring. And that's when I realize…I *know* that wedding ring. I know that ratty blue nightgown.

"Mom…?" I whisper.

At first, the woman doesn't register that I'm there. My voice wavers. "*Mom?*"

The woman reels around, startling me. Her face is matted with blood. It takes me a moment to realize that, yes, this is my mother, and yes, she is in pain, and *yes*, her eyes are gone. *Her eyes are gone.* Empty sockets stare back at me, gnarled optic nerves dangling down her cheeks.

Her hands reach towards me. She holds small mangled orbs in her outstretched palms. Her eyes. She's offering me her eyes. "It's too much," my mother says. "Too much."

I back up, the light in the bathroom blinding me. My mother comes closer. I stumble back. No escape. I'm moving so slowly, like I'm running through water.

Run, Ange, run.

But I can't. I can't move. And that's when I shoot up with a gasp. Sweating. Clutching my chest.

Oh, God. It takes me a few seconds to realize I'm still in my bed and that it's morning. Two sparrows chirp outside the window on a lone tree branch.

It was just a dream. Just a dream.

Catching my breath, my eyes drift over to the mesh-wire trashcan where I've abandoned my empty prescription bottle. Is this how it's going to be? Are blood and death in my future? I pick up the photo of my mother. I never noticed it before, but there's something disquieting about how she's sitting. As if she's performing for the picture taker, for my father. It's her eyes. Her eyes are full of fear.

The realization that my mother is terrified in this photograph washes over me. My mother is afraid. She has no future. And I'm feeling more and more like her everyday. Maybe Jackson's right. Maybe I do have to face my fears head-on. Prove once and for all that I'm my own person, and if not, if that doesn't work, then take the money and run. I've taken care of a lot of my debt. If this elderly woman pays double our rate, my cut would last months. I could get out of here. Get away from Jackson. From home.

Rubbing my face, I try to erase the image of my mother's eyes and how they looked like bloody golf balls. Inanimate *things*. The sun trickles through the window, soft and bright. I pull the covers off the bed. My bare feet touch the hard floor.

I nudge Jackson's bedroom door open. *Don't do it,* a small voice whispers inside of me. *Turn back.* But I push that voice down, burying it deep within me. Beth blinks awake and sees me standing there. She pulls the sheets over her naked chest.

"Babe…" she says, sleep in her voice.

"Huh?" Jackson yawns and wraps his arms around her. It's only when he opens his eyes that he sees me standing in the doorway. No more fear. No more hiding.

"I'm in," I say.

5

It's the type of fall day where the world is wide and open. Our car cruises down the narrow highway. Golden leaves flutter past the windows. Beth rides up front with Jackson like always, and I sit in the back with Elliot. Every now and then, Jackson will glance down at his phone and curse. He's looking at the map of town, but the picture's not fully loading. We drive deeper into the woods. Jackson slows, making a U-turn.

"You should have made a right back there," Beth says.

"I know where it is."

"Where the hell are you taking us?" Elliot asks jokingly, trying to lighten the mood. Everyone's tense. We all know where we're going. Elliot tweaks the circuit board on his EMF meter. "Shoot," he says. His tools bounce on the seat. I hold them in place.

Jackson glances back at us. "It's not working?"

"Not since our last gig."

"Won't even turn on?"

"It turns on. Just…I had it rigged to give false readings, right?"

"Yeah."

"But the circuit I built came loose again and now I can't…" Elliot struggles with the wires. He pushes too far, and the tool slips from his hand. "Yeah. It's done for. Damn it."

In the distance, smeared black clouds appear on the horizon. I think of the girls that disappeared from the Cypress Street house. I think of the old lady still there. What does she do with her days? How does she stand being in that house all alone?

We turn left, making our way towards the gathering storm. It isn't long before rain collects on the windshield. Jackson pops some pills as he drives. I exchange a look with Elliot. Beth pretends not to notice.

"How much further?" Jackson asks.

Beth looks at her phone. "Can't tell. No bars now."

"Me neither," Jackson says.

"I've got one bar," I say.

"Try calling, would you?" Jackson says.

"Here's the number." Beth hands me the digits on a small piece of paper.

Jackson drums his hands on the wheel. "Tell her we just passed marker 37."

I punch in the numbers and hold the phone to my ear. It rings. Once. Twice. Then, there's a click. Hissing. No one speaks.

"Hello?" I ask.

More static. A tiny voice crackles through. It's barely

discernible, like a small child giggling. *Impossible*, I think. There are no small children in the house. "Is anyone…?"

Suddenly, a horrible shriek erupts from the phone. I pull the phone away, wincing.

"What?" Jackson asks.

"You sure that's the right number?"

Beth shrugs. "That's what she gave us."

There's a low rumbling in my stomach. Feeling nauseous, I crack a window.

"What're you doing? It's raining," Jackson says.

Droplets fall on the car seat. "Just need some air," I say, positioning my face near the crack. The cool wind helps a little, but not much. Elliot eyes me curiously, but doesn't say anything.

"Wait," Beth says. She leans forward. "What's that?"

Up ahead, situated deep in an overgrown field, is a sprawling house. Grime clings to the outside of the façade, and the grass is tall and thick, swaying gently in the breeze. The building almost looks like it could have been beautiful once upon a time, but now it's just decrepit. Ornaments clutter the yard, and a wire fence and wrought-iron gate encircle the property. On the lawn, a middle-aged Hispanic man prunes a pair of half-alive shrubs with rusty shears.

Jackson pulls the car into the rain ravaged dirt driveway. Rain pelts down. He parks. Waiting. Everyone looks up at the house.

"It's bigger in person," Elliot says.

"It's going to be hell running wire through it," Beth says.

"We supposed to walk?" I ask.

"She said it's be open," Jackson replies. He squints

through the windshield and then lays on the horn. The sound echoes through the rain-soaked afternoon. The gardener doesn't even turn his head. "What the hell?" Jackson fidgets in his seat. After a second or two, he pops another pill. Beth tenses beside him.

"Can I have some?" I ask.

Jackson snorts.

"Maybe take it easy," Beth says.

Jackson smiles. "Have to put on the charm, don't I?"

Beth purses her lips, about to say something, but then shakes her head. There's a distant rumble of thunder. I study the lawn ornaments on the other side of the gate. They're positioned in scenes: elves eating around a table, bunnies lined up in a row, fairy creatures dancing. My gaze drifts off. In the distance, I catch sight of a tiny figure past the house.

I wipe the car window's glass with my hand. The figure is small and shadowed, but from here it looks like a child. Long hair matted down in the rain. Pressing closer to the window, I try to get a better look. The child faces me and wears a long dress. I blink a few times, wondering if my mind's playing tricks on me again. After a moment, she turns and scurries off. Growing smaller. I try to locate her between the trees, hoping to catch a glimpse of her face.

Wham.

Without warning, a brown mass slams the window in front of me. I yelp and pull back. Everyone jumps. On the other side of the glass, a clawing, slobbering German Shepherd snarls at me. I glare through the window, giving the dog the finger.

"Stupid dog."

We watch the dog trot in circles and then head back the way it came. It slips through the bars of the gate towards a hunched over silhouette. Leaning on a cane, the silhouette journeys across the endless lawn.

"Is that her?" Beth asks. She scrunches her nose. The silhouette pulls out a heavy ring of keys. She works a rusty old key into the massive iron gate and tugs. It falls open with a loud squeak. Then she lifts a hand and waves us through.

"Okay then," Jackson says. He puts the car into drive. It sloshes towards the house. The iron gate creaks shut behind us. Up close the building consists of crumbled bricks and chipped paint. Weathered stone cherub statues guard the doors. It looks like there's never been any sort of restoration to the property. I wonder about the children who slept behind these walls, what it was like to live here. Everything about the house seems broken.

Jackson rolls up to the circular driveway just as lightning flashes in the distance.

"That's just perfect," I say, eyeing the sky.

"Unload?" Elliot asks Jackson, nodding to the equipment.

"Let's scout it out first," Jackson says.

The hunched silhouette hobbles onto the porch. We exchange wary looks.

"Anyone else feel like we're about to get raped?" Beth asks.

Yes, I want to say, but I keep quiet. The gate's already closed. It would be too much trouble to go back now. Jackson climbs out of the car. We follow him into the wall of rain, scrambling up the uneven cobblestone steps.

"Careful," Elliot says. "It's slick."

I almost fall backwards, but manage to catch myself. The rain slicker clad silhouette steps into the house. The others follow her, and after one last look to the lawn ornaments and the gardener, I do too.

Inside, Mrs. Green shakes off her jacket, revealing her broad-shoulders and hunched back. She looks to be in the mid-60s and has these tired, sad eyes. A gnarly scar travels from the corner of her mouth to her ear.

The German Shepherd runs up to us, fur wet, and sniffs our jackets and pants. He prods his nose into my leg, throwing me off balance.

"*Sebastian*. No. Outside. *Outside*," Mrs. Green says, pointing to the door.

The dog cowers, tail between its legs, and then sulks outside.

"Shoes off please. Just mopped." She smiles, hanging up her rain slicker.

We remove our shoes. The antique furniture looks like it hasn't been used in decades. The curtains are closed on every window, and there's a damp, sweet smell, like rotting garbage. I run my hand along a chair and a layer of fine dust cakes on my fingers. Wiping the dust on my jeans, I study a portrait of a stern lady, her hands clasped on her lap.

"That isn't me," Mrs. Green says. She pulls down her dress, which has risen over her thighs, revealing a beige slip. "It's my mother. She was a looker, wasn't she?" She chuckles.

I smile. "She was."

"Now, which one of you is Jackson?" she says.

Jackson holds out his hand. "Mrs. Green? That would be me. We spoke on the phone." This is where Jackson's on his best behavior, when he's introducing us to new clients. Mrs. Green seems flustered with his direct gaze, and I'm reminded how charming my brother can be.

"Oh. Pleasure to meet you. So handsome."

"Well, thank you. Not so bad yourself."

As Jackson does his thing, I can't help staring at the vaulted ceiling and the oil paintings of gleeful children. They gaze down at me, their eyes bright and hopeful. Does anyone else find this creepy? But no, the gang's focused on Jackson.

I walk over to a sepia-toned photograph of the house's first construction. As if on cue, ringing drifts through my ears. I think back to what Jackson said when I was a kid: "It's all in your little head, Ange. Don't be like Mom."

But I am like her, more than he or I will ever admit. The ringing is barely audible. It taunts me, drifting louder and louder. *I'm not crazy.* I squeeze my eyes shut, trying to breathe in and out like normal people do.

Abruptly, the ringing stops. I open my eyes. Mrs. Green smiles cordially, the garden of wrinkles stretching across her face. "Would anyone care for some tea?"

Although Mrs. Green is here alone, the kitchen's disarray still surprises me. The trash overflows with uneaten food and flies circle the moldy counter. "Sorry for the mess," Mrs. Green says. "I fell a few months ago. Ever since things haven't been the same."

We stand awkwardly as Mrs. Green clatters around the sink, moving cups, fixing a pot of tea. There's a plate of cookies on the counter. A fat cockroach scurries across the cooked dough, disappearing behind a pile of dishes. Mrs.

Green picks up the plate. She hobbles over to the table and motions for us to sit down. "Here we are," she says. "Little under-baked. How the girls used to like 'em."

"Hey. Underbaked. That's the way to go," Jackson says.

We all slouch in the rickety chairs. As Mrs. Green sits down, she winces. "Oof. Old bones." She nods to Elliot. "My dear, I may need you to go get the water when the whistle goes. Don't ever get old. None of you."

She digs out a plastic case that holds her false teeth. I try not to watch as she pops them in and smacks her gums together. Elliot grimaces besides me. Beth clears her throat.

"Help yourselves," Mrs. Green says. She bites into a cookie, crumbs clinging to her lips. We offer wide, placating smiles.

"Oh. No, thanks," Elliot says.

"I'm good," Beth chimes.

"Watching my figure." Jackson looks away.

Mrs. Green deflates a little. I wait for someone to give in, but when no one does, I lean forward. "I'll have one," I say, reaching for the smallest cookie. Mrs. Green beams as I take a nibble, and when I notice a tiny crinkly hair protruding from a chocolate chip I try not to cringe.

"Mmm. Delicious," I say. "Thank you."

"Did you have any trouble finding the place?" Mrs. Green asks.

"Nope," Jackson replies. "Nice plot of land you've got here."

"It really is a beautiful house," I say, rapping my knuckles against the flowered wallpaper.

"Quite a handful," Mrs. Green says. "Used to have a maid,

landscapers…but now it's just Manuel. Part of me wants to say 'to heck with it.' Leave it all behind. But I bought this house with my husband, before the war. It's the only thing I have left of his. Plus, with its history, it's not an easy sell."

She forces a weary laugh. Jackson gives a plastic little chuckle as he reaches into his backpack. *Don't do it,* I think. *Don't be that crass.* But he takes out the invoice and slides it across the table.

"Yeah, so, speaking of…um, this is what we agreed to," he says.

"Yes." Mrs. Green takes out her spectacles. "Of course. After the job is done. Correct?"

Jackson hesitates.

"That's what it says on your website. Satisfaction guaranteed?"

"You found our website?" Beth asks.

"Of course," Mrs. Green replies. "Why do you ask? Surprised I know how to surf the web?"

Beth shrugs, not sure what to say.

"I'm geriatric. Not *Jurassic*," Mrs. Green says, chuckling at her own joke. We chuckle along with her.

"So, yeah. Anyway…we guarantee you'll be satisfied," Jackson says.

Mrs. Green nods. "My situation. It's rather unique."

"You said…you hear screaming?" I ask.

"The girls," Mrs. Green says, her face darkening. "It's been twenty-five years since we discovered what my Herman did. They never managed to find him, as you know. Sometimes I think, if only I had caught it early. He was a curious child. Prone to fits. More than once I found him spying on the girls.

I just never thought…well, he's long gone now. I tried to keep things as they were. A memorial of sorts. After my accident though, I've just been so tired."

Mrs. Green pauses. Her fragile old eyes water. It's so quiet I can hear her swallow. "That's when the voices crept in. Just whispers at first. Then giggles and snickers. And I'd…I'd just tell myself, 'Martha, you're getting batty in your old age'."

Blinking slowly, she makes a small clearing sound in her throat. "But lately…all they do is scream. I try turning up the television. But it's no use. I haven't slept a whole night through."

The sudden sharp whistle of the teakettle blows steam behind us. I sit on my hands and try not to show that I'm rattled. Elliot hops up to fetch the water.

"Just bring it over with that tray, please," Mrs. Green says. "And the sugar bowl. That little piggy. On the counter."

Elliot gathers everything as Mrs. Green studies me. I shift under her gaze. "You're the one with the gift," she says. After a long moment, I nod.

"I read about your mother. I'm sorry," Mrs. Green says.

"Thanks. It's okay," I say.

"Mine, she had her demons. I spent the better part of my teens in a home just like this one. How I ended up here. My husband made sure I was well provided for. It was only right to give back. To help those like me."

Her lips quiver. Tears form in her baggy, sleepless eyes. "But I failed them. I failed those girls."

I reach out and touch her old withered hand. It feels like crinkled newspaper under mine.

"Has anyone else heard the screaming?" I ask. "The gardener?"

"Manuel? No. It…happens at night. Those poor things."

Jackson hides his impatience with a concerned nod. "And the bodies. I know it's hard, but where were the girls discovered? Knowing will help us with the investigation."

Mrs. Green's eyes glaze over, remembering. She swallows. "Yes, well, Herman…he was quite messy. He hid bits. Some in the pond. Others in closets. The attic. Cupboards. The police tried to piece the girls together, but there were always *gaps*."

A heavy silence falls over the kitchen.

"It wasn't your fault," I say to Mrs. Green. "I'm sure they know that."

Mrs. Green's face crumbles. She looks earnestly at me. "Please. Just make it stop," she says. "All I want is a quiet house."

6

I avoid being alone with Jackson throughout the routine sweep of the house, although as soon as Mrs. Green excuses herself to check on Manuel, Jackson grabs my shoulder. Elliot and Beth come closer.

"Did you see her hands?" Elliot asks. "They were shaking."

"We're all going to hell," Beth says.

"Or being reincarnated as maggots," I reply.

"Funny," Jackson replies. "Let's just remember why we're all here. Now, Green says to stay away from the East Hall due to decay, so that helps us some, but we need to pick our staging areas carefully. This place is a beast. If we're not careful, we'll wind up staying until Friday trying to make this feel legit."

"I think we should monitor down in the den," Beth says, fixing her hair in a ponytail. "Easiest to run cable to."

"Good. And you pulled those new sounds, right?"

She holds up her phone and presses a button. The giggling of little children plays softly.

"Beautiful," Jackson says.

"*And*…wait for it." Beth presses play again. The sound morphs to little girls screaming. It's sick, but you have to hand it to Beth, she can be very inventive.

"Love it," Jackson smiles. "Okay, so Babe, I'll give you the tap when it's time. First we'll do the giggling. Then we'll amp it up from there."

"Sure," Beth says.

"Ange," Jackson says. "Same as last time. I'll cue your walkie with two clicks. That means Mrs. Green has heard the giggling and you need to react."

I nod, only half listening, and test a loose floorboard with my foot. This whole house feels like it's going to fall apart.

"Earth to Ange," Jackson says.

"Got it," I say.

Next to me, Elliot's EMF meter chirps. He takes it out of his pocket. The ticker bounces a little. Elliot's brow furrows.

Jackson surveys the team. "We need to act like we're making contact with multiple entities, right?" he says. "So milk the shit out of it. Maybe I can even get some extra dough out of her."

He continues talking a mile a minute. I nod in the appropriate pauses, but then a sharp, aching pain shoots across my forehead. *Oh, no.* Slowly, the ringing noise returns, drifting into my ears and drowning out my brother's voice. I squint. Ringing means my mind is on the fritz, either that or death's coming.

But that's impossible. It's just me. Just crazy.

I stop walking. Maybe if I stand still nothing will happen, but even as I think this, I can tell that there's something close by, watching us from the hallway.

Turning, I peer down the long, windowless corridor. After a few moments, the outline of a small child appears. I can make out a flower-print dress and tangled hair. Tucked under her arm is a ratty teddy bear, and her hands cover her mouth like she has a dirty secret.

I stop in my tracks. It's the same little girl. The one I saw outside, by the woods. From this angle, she looks albino, her face and hair devoid of color. The longer I stare, the louder the ringing grows. She stands there, unmoving, staring right back at me.

"You got all that, sis?" Jackson asks. He's been talking all this time, but I haven't heard a word. The ringing swells. "Ange," Jackson says. "*Ange.*"

I break my gaze from the albino girl and look at Jackson. When I glance back down the hall, she's gone.

"The hell's wrong with you? " Jackson asks.

"Nothing," I reply, inspecting the wooden walls for hidden rooms where the girl might be hiding.

"Alright," Jackson says, giving me a long look. "Let's get to work then. Get in, get out. Remember?"

"Ange, your…" Elliot gestures to my nose. I wipe my nostril. Blood smears on my hand. I step back, acting like it's no big deal. Jackson studies the blood. He narrows his eyes, knowing something isn't right.

"I'll be right back," I say, hurrying down the hall.

•　　•　　•

In the master bathroom, mildew tiles and a row of low sinks line one side of the wall. I move to the first sink and turn the knob. It whines with rust before murky water dribbles out. I wait for the water to become clear and then splash some on my nostrils. Still trembling, I eye my reflection in the warped, cloudy mirror.

"You're okay, Ange," I say. "You're okay. You're…"

Behind me, I hear feet pad softly on the tiles. I startle, spinning around, just in time to see a shadow quickly flit by. Scanning the bathroom, I step away from the sink.

"Ange."

I jump, but it's just Elliot. "Jesus."

"Sorry. Wanted to…make sure you were all right."

"Thanks. Yeah. I'm fine."

We share an awkward silence, but then I hear a faint whimpering behind Elliot. It echoes over the tiles. I turn back to the row of stalls. Mold and cobwebs frame the doors. The whimpering is soft, like a little girl crying. It's coming from the last stall.

"What's wrong?" Elliot asks.

"You don't hear that?" I reply.

He shakes his head. I close my eyes, but the stifled cries only grow into raking sobs. There's no way to shut them out. I steel myself and move down the row.

"Ange?" Elliot asks.

"Shh," I reply. He follows cautiously behind me. The ticker on Elliot's EMF meter bounces. Gentle, this time. Intermittent. He studies the EMF meter and gives me a worried glance.

The whimpering grows louder as we delve closer,

creeping along the chipped linoleum. Elliot tries to make out the EMF meter reading. The needle spikes. "That's impossible," he says.

When we're at the door to the last stall, the sobbing ends abruptly. Through the dim light, I make out the rusty door handle. Rain pitters on the skylight. The sound's almost soothing. I try to breathe deeply, but only manage steady, shallow breaths. My quivering hand taps the door. It yawns open with a rickety squeak.

But there's nothing but a rust-stained toilet on the other side. I share a shaky smile with Elliot. My heart rate slows.

"You want to get out of here?" he says.

"Please. Let's get this over with."

We walk to the exit. Right as we're about to step into the hallway, the first stall door groans open.

"What the…?" Elliot says.

The whimpering picks up again. Crystal clear. But Elliot doesn't hear it. Slowly, I move towards the stall. A thought suddenly occurs to me: What if everything my mother told me growing up was real? And all this time Jackson and my father were wrong? That would mean spirits secretly walked among us. It's a simple thought I've rejected all my life, that my mother may have been right, but in this moment with Elliot it feels inexplicably true.

I round the corner, peeking into the stall…

A wave of relief washes over me. There's nothing there. Thank God, there's nothing there. I laugh at the absurdity of it all. "It's empty," I say. "Completely empty."

"You are really freaking me out," Elliot says.

A stupid grin plasters on my face. *Thank you, thank you,*

thank you, I think. But my relief doesn't last long. Soon, a dark mass appears behind Elliot. It's a bulging shadow that only comes up to his thighs. A little girl.

She's crouched behind Elliot, facing away from us, a lopsided bow in her hair.

"Oh, no…" I whisper.

Elliot studies me. "What?" He looks around. "What now?"

The pale, chubby legs of the girl quiver as she slowly turns. I pull Elliot into the stall, stretching his shirt, and slam the door behind us. We stand in the cramped space, so close I can smell the spearmint from his gum.

"Ange? What did you see?" Elliot asks.

Lightning shatters the darkness. Once. Twice. It illuminates the stall for a moment, but it's enough time to see that we're not alone. *She's* found us. That pudgy girl stands on the toilet, hunched over, inches away. Her face is by my torso, her cheeks smeared in blood.

Go away, I think. *I don't want this, and I don't want you.* The pudgy girl crouches down, prepared to pounce, but just before she does, just before I think I might die if she touches me, the room spins. My knees buckle, and I feel a tingling and then gushing from my nose.

I see the wall, the ceiling, and then the floor.

And then I'm somewhere else…

Somewhere bright and warm. And I'm not alone. My mother's with me, and she's wearing a long flowing peasant dress, the one she used to wear to readings, and she's laughing. She's telling me to come closer, into the nothingness behind her. There are outlines of trees and grass and creatures around us, or maybe it's the wind? There are no shadows here.

Just the quiet of wherever we are.

A voice, tinny and muddled, breaks through the silence.

My mother furrows her brow. No. Wait.

She's trying to tell me something. She's disappearing, the brightness taking over, washing out her face, her lips. She's speaking fast, but there's no sound. No words. I have so much to ask her. I have so many questions. But I can't talk. There's nothing here. No sound. No pain.

"Ange. *Ange.*"

I'm being torn away. The pull overwhelms me, tearing at my ribs, my legs. No. Please.

"Can you hear me?"

I like the emptiness. Let me stay. Just a little while longer. The brightness is gone now. Cold bombards my skin, seeping into my blood. I'm aware of my hands. They're shaking.

"Ange. That's it. Come on."

Through the blinding haze, there are shadows, and through these shadows, there is Jackson. He's gently resting his hand on my neck, feeling my pulse. There's genuine concern in his eyes.

Blinking a few times, I feel the solid, hard linoleum floor on my back. I'm in the bathroom again. Jackson breathes deeply. "Man, Ange. I swear…" His voice trails off.

Beth and Elliot appear beside him. Rough paper scratches the skin under my nose. Beth presses toilet paper to my nostrils, trying to stem the bleeding.

The bleeding. *I'm* bleeding. Slowly, I sit up.

Elliot places a hand on my back for support. "Careful," Elliot says.

"Here," Beth says, handing me another wad of tissues. I struggle to get my bearings as Jackson studies me.

"What happened?" he asks.

I try to stand taller so everyone won't look so worried, but the room keeps spinning.

"You need to sit down?" Jackson asks.

"I'm…"

Jackson cracks his knuckles. He nods to Elliot. "So, what is this? Don't keep us in the dark. She was on the ground. Hardly breathing."

Elliot thinks about this, then he shrugs. "Said she heard something. And then she just…I don't know. Cashed out."

"I'm *okay*," I say, wobbling on my feet. Elliot catches me, and our eyes lock for a fleeting moment.

"Look," Elliot says. "Maybe we should come back another time."

"She said she's fine," Jackson says.

"She just passed out," Elliot counters.

Jackson doesn't say anything.

"Just got a little woozy," I say. "When I saw my own blood. Seriously. I'm okay." I force a smile. Although I know Jackson doesn't believe me for a second, he still claps his hands, ready for business.

"Okay. Good," Jackson says. "Let's get back to it then."

"We should talk about this," Elliot replies.

"She said she's fine." With one last look to me, Jackson disappears out the door. Beth hesitates like she's going to say something, but then stops herself. "You know he loves you, right?"

I shrug. "Sure."

She takes in my standoffish stance and then follows Jackson out the door.

At the sink, I dab the toilet paper under the faucet and wipe away the remaining bloody smears on my skin. Elliot lingers behind me. I know he has questions, but I don't know how to answer them.

"You don't have to do this, you know? If you're not feeling…" Elliot says.

"I know," I reply.

"And you don't have to let him push you around like that."

"I need to do this, El. The money's good. You know it."

"Is that you talking or Jackson?"

"I can't wait any longer," I say. "I have to face this."

"Face what?" Elliot asks.

"Face…" I struggle to find the right words. "Face me. Face what's inside of me. I don't want to end up like Mom."

"You've never really talked about it," he says.

"Not sure I know how."

"I'm here. If you ever need someone."

"Thanks," I say, trying to be strong. "But I'm fine. Really. Come on. Let's get this over with."

Elliot studies me for a moment, and then nods. I watch him walk away, not wanting to admit how much it means to me that he's the last to go.

In the foyer, we lug equipment through the rain-slick doorway. Mrs. Green peruses an old shelf. When I approach her, she taps the dusty glass of a clock. "It's strange," she says. "Having people here is making me see this place in a new light." She looks at me with those sad eyes.

This is the part I really hate, though it's necessary for what we do. "So, um…I was wondering if you might have some photos," I say.

"Photos?"

"Of the girls. Something I could use to identify them."

Mrs. Green blinks at me. She smiles slowly. "Yes. Of course," she says.

We sit in the kitchen, at the long table with years of caked grime and crumbs. Mrs. Green rifles through photo albums. Children smile in the pictures, running around on a grassy lawn.

"Are these foster kids of yours, or family?" I ask.

"Oh, just friends along the way. People always coming and going. This was before the whispers. Before everything. You know, it's not only voices. There are visions too. I saw someone, right over here." She points to a cabinet full of glasses. "It was late at night. I heard laughter."

"But no whispering?" I ask.

"It was an awful racket. I took my cane and went around the bend. There was this little girl. This odd little girl."

"Can you describe her?"

"She wasn't looking at me, but out the door, just staring at the backyard, and then she…tangled."

"Tangled?" I ask.

"Her limbs. She bent down and kept bending in places she shouldn't have been. It was all quite dreadful."

In my notebook, I scribble imaginary notes, trying to make sense of it. "Any more incidents on the first floor? More visions?"

"Just there." Mrs. Green points to the space before the cabinet. Her fingers travel over the photo album. She turns the pages and then struggles to lift out a photograph midway through the book.

On the table, she lays out an old crinkled photograph of herself posed with twelve stern young girls in front of the house. I scan the two rows. Each girl has their hair braided in neat little braids. Most of the girls' expressions mimic Mrs. Green's stern face, though some try to smile.

My eyes drift to the first row. *The albino girl and the fat girl.* I've seen those two before. Mrs. Green hands me a pen. She nudges the photo my way. "You can write on this one," she says. "I have plenty."

I take the ballpoint pen and uncap it. Mrs. Green drags her bony finger across the photo, pointing to the fat girl.

"There's Missy," she says. I scribble the name next to the photo.

"The tall one's Tammy," Mrs. Green continues, tapping the picture where an awkwardly tall, gangly girl grins for the camera. She wears leg laces, but despite her handicap, she has a patient face.

"Then there's Claire…" Mrs. Green continues. She takes in a slight breath and points to the petite albino girl. It's the spitting image of the pale little girl I've seen around the house. I write *Claire* above the girl's head. "She was the first to go missing," Mrs. Green says. "Poor thing. Someone left her on our doorstep in a basket when she was just a week old. She was so ill. The nurses, none of them thought she'd live to see her first birthday, but…she was a fighter, that Claire."

Mrs. Green runs a sullen finger over the picture. Tears well in her droopy eyes. I look away, training my gaze on the photo, and notice a hulking young man raking leaves underneath a tree. His face is concealed in shadows.

"And him?" I ask.

Mrs. Green's expression hardens. She eyes me curiously. "That's Herman, my dear. He's long gone."

The Herman. The one who took those poor girls and made them scream. A wave of nausea rolls over me. I hesitate and then write *Herman* next to his body.

The rain batters the frail frame of the house. From the den, I peer out the window. Puddles pool on the lawn. The courtyard pond overflows onto the grass. We've been here for a few hours, but it feels like days.

Beth boots up the computers and then flips on the monitors. Various rooms of the house light up on the screens in black and white. Mrs. Green sits primly beside Beth, while Jackson's sprawled on the other side. They're all keenly observing, all playing their parts.

"Yeah, so…" Jackson scratches behind his ear. "First, Angela's going to do a full sweep of the house. Every room. It can take some time, but once she establishes contact, and trust…she'll ask them one by one to leave."

"It must be lovely," Mrs. Green says. "Working with family. Having them close."

Jackson smirks. "Gotta love it. Even if they drive you crazy."

"Alright guys. All feeds are live. Ready on this end," Beth says.

Mrs. Green remains fixed on Jackson. Never blinking. She looks between my brother and me. "She inherited the gift," Mrs. Green says. "From your mother?"

"Mmhmm," Jackson replies.

"Why didn't you?" she asks.

It's an innocent question, but her directness catches Jackson off guard. He smiles wide, searching for the right words. "Recessive gene. Sort of thing. I guess," he says.

Nearby, Elliot has the back of the EMF meter open again, examining the circuits. There's this concerned look he gets when dismantling a machine that I find incredibly endearing. I envy him, because he can work on something with total concentration whereas I can't focus on anything, and when I can it's usually someone or *something* I don't want to see.

Jackson wheels around in his chair. "You ready to go?" There's a note of urgency in his voice. Mrs. Green studies Elliot. He methodically puts the EMF meter back together again. "Ready."

Jackson smiles assuredly at Mrs. Green. She tilts her head.

"Let's go," I say to Elliot, heading away from Beth's computers. He picks up the video camera and clicks it on.

We walk steadily down the hallway, the lights flickering on and off with the thunder. "May lose power," Elliot says.

"Let's hope not," I reply, clicking my walkie. "Can you see anything?" I ask Beth.

Her voice crackles through the device. "Too dark on the monitors. Try night viz."

Elliot flips a switch. He gives me the thumbs up sign.

"Better," Beth says. Elliot nods, adjusting the levels, and then kills the camera. It's so fast I don't pick up on it at first. He walks right up to me, until we're inches away from each other's faces, and looks me in the eyes. "The EMF meter. In the bathroom," he says. "It was moving. Like…a lot."

I glance away. "Cause you rigged it."

"No. I never fixed the false circuit. The reading was legit." He grabs my arm when I try to step back. "You saw something," he continues. "Come on, Ange."

"What? No." I try to squirm away from him.

Beth's voice splinters through the walkie. "You guys ready? Elliot?"

But Elliot doesn't pick up the camera. "What was it?"

he asks. "What did you see? You don't have to carry this inside."

I swallow hard, weighing my options. Here's this guy, asking me wholeheartedly what's wrong, and I don't even have the decency to tell him the truth?

Beth's impatient voice crackles through the walkie. "Elliot? Ange? You copy?"

We stare at the walkie. "You wouldn't believe me if I told you," I say.

Elliot nods. "Yeah. Maybe," he replies. "The thing is, Ange, Jackson can talk all he wants about how your mom was crazy, and maybe that's his way to deal, and maybe he really believes what he's saying, but life isn't that black and white. There's a lot in this world we don't understand. A lot in this world we *can't* understand."

"My mom *was* crazy, El. She slit her wrists."

"I'm just saying," Elliot says, and what he says next, he says very slowly. "Maybe, just maybe, all these years later, it wouldn't be so bad to consider the possibility that life is all kinds of grey, and that your mom might have been dialed into something that was beyond all of us."

I feel as if I've been punched in the throat. Having Elliot articulate what I've been thinking solidifies my gut instinct in a way that's hard to ignore. I try to keep calm.

"I'm not saying you have to believe it," Elliot says. "But at least consider there may be something else at play."

"Didn't take you for a believer," I reply.

"Me neither." Elliot smiles.

"He-llo?" Beth's static-filled voice rings out between us. "Guys?"

"Yeah," I say. "Copy."

"Tell Elliot to check his feed. We're in the dark here."

Elliot gives my hand a squeeze. He searches my face. I've done so well to cover up my feelings over the years, I know he won't find any answers there, but the fact that he's looking lights a small, pulsing hope in my chest.

I hold up the walkie. "Starting in the North hall."

Walking down the corridor, I picture Mrs. Green leaning forward with Jackson and Beth as they watch the monitors. No doubt Jackson will be playing up the magnificence of my gift, how I've changed so many lives, how I can transform Mrs. Green's world, too. Elliot's footsteps pad softly behind me. I try to stand up straighter for the camera, to pretend that I know what I'm doing.

We enter a study with tiny combo desks overrun with cobwebs. It's a long ignored space, and a thick coating of dust clings to every surface. I hold onto my flashlight like a lifeline, letting the rakish light illuminate the walls.

When I come to an old slate chalkboard, I slow down. The board's smudged with tiny fingerprints. Smeared in old chalk across the dark slate is one word…

Shhhhhh.

Elliot maneuvers around the desks to get a better shot. Dread blooms inside me. Jackson's voice crackles through the speakers. "Ange, you feeling anything in there?"

I turn in a full circle, sweeping the light across the empty desks. "Nothing," I say.

"Let's keep moving. Lots of ground to cover tonight," Jackson says. His crackly voice fills the room.

"Copy that," I reply.

The next room we enter has rows of bunk beds with long untouched mattresses. I drag the light over the walls, illuminating timeworn paintings and sketches. On paper, colorful stick figure children play. Green for grass. Blue for sky.

Taking another step, my foot kicks something. I stop and kneel down, finding a small cloth lump. A ragged doll. When I shine the flashlight on the face, its mouth has been stitched shut.

I exchange a quick look with Elliot. Right as our eyes lock, a sque-eak echoes behind us. Whirling around, I can detect the sound comes from the hallway. Sque-eak. Sque-eak.

Like a rusted joint.

Sque-eak.

I set the doll down and move back towards the hallway. "Please tell me you hear that," I say, but when I drag the light over Elliot's face, he only looks bewildered. He's about to say something, but the sque-eak picks up again. I shush him and inch towards the hallway.

Sque-eak. Sque-eak.

Elliot follows behind me, the light from the flashlight daggering through the darkness. His walkie crackles. Jackson's voice flows through the tiny speakers: "El, where's she going?"

"Not sure," Elliot replies.

Sque-eak.

I rush down the hall, through an open doorway, into a library filled with worn books. Flashing the light on the high ceilings, I study the delicate light sconces and the photos of playing children. When Elliot tells me to stop, I keep moving, searching, listening. I walk to the rows of books, but there's no sound. I'm about to step back outside when I hear a whining sque-eak. It's rusty and close. Urgent.

Lumbering footsteps now accompany the sound. I halt, and then move closer. Something ruffles on the other side of the shelf, but I've seen enough horror movies to not want to look.

Elliot grows restless behind me. "You see anything?" he asks.

I shake my head. On the lower shelf, I remove a book with a cracked leather spine, leaving an inch wide hole to the other side. Leaning forward, I scan the open space, but all I see are more books and a lone air vent.

"There's nothing there," I say, relieved.

But then a small-boned figure drifts past on the other side. I stumble back into Elliot. "Woah," he says. "You okay?"

Jackson's impatient voice cuts through the darkness: "Ange, what's going on?"

I hold up the walkie. "There's something here," I say.

"You think you can make contact?" he replies.

"Of course," I reply, even though I'm not sure.

There's a strange look on Elliot's face. He reaches into his bag and pulls out his EMF meter. The meter flutters out of control, the pin-like needle dancing wildly. The squeaking returns on the other side of the bookcase.

"You really don't hear that?" I ask.

Elliot shakes his head. I steady myself, prowling around the corner to the next row. At first, I see nothing, but then that ringing noise knifes in and out of my ears. Down the row, in a shallow doorway, is a tall, gangly silhouette. With trembling hands, I reach in my back pocket and unfold the crinkled photo of the girls. Glancing at the names and the girls' faces, I pinpoint the one with the leg braces.

"Tammy," I whisper, reading off the written name of the girl.

Her cumbersome frame lumbers off in those squeaking leg braces. I follow her.

"Ange, where are you going?" Elliot says. "Come on. Give me something."

Down the hallway, I watch Tammy awkwardly totter with her leg braces. I say her name louder, though my voice catches. "*Tammy.*"

She halts, balancing on her braces. I try to control the ringing in my ears. Slowly, Tammy turns, her face obscured in shadows. I can feel her staring at me. The ringing daggers in my head. "Tammy. My name's Angela…"

Tammy raises a finger to her lips. "Shhh," she says, giving me a long look.

She then pivots, her metal braces creaking as she clomps down the hall. Sque-eak. Sque-eak. Sque-eak. Elliot stands next to me, filming the hallway, and then my reaction.

"You're not seeing this?" I ask.

He shakes his head again, his eyes wide. I stare after Tammy. "She wants us to follow her," I say.

Elliot drops the camera a little. "Okay," he replies, his voice unsure. Steeling myself, I carry on down the hall.

The walkie dips in and out with static. "Ange, you copy?" Jackson says. "Turn back. Mrs. Green says the girls never went in the East Hall."

But I keep going. Elliot shifts behind me. "We should turn around."

A rotting floorboard groans under my foot. "Turn around then," I say.

"Ange, come on. You're freaking me out."

Tammy's disappeared around a corner now. The floorboards creak under us like cracking ice. "I just, I feel like…we're almost there," I say, and it's true. It's like we're on the verge of something. The air crackles with electricity.

"Almost…where?" he asks. "I'm all for you following your gut, but you can't keep me in the dark." When I say nothing, he sighs. "Let's…"

There's a sickening *shunk* behind me.

Looking back, I see floorboards splintering and the last of Elliot plummeting down into darkness. The sound of a deep thud, like a sack of rocks hitting concrete, echoes up from wherever he lands. "Elliot!" I call out, rushing to the broken floor.

Jackson's walkie is on, and I can hear the commotion in the den. Mrs. Green's voice blends with Beth's and Jackson's. Questions echo back at me: "Did Elliot trip? Why is it so dark? Where are you? Hello? Where *are* you?"

Jackson's voice cuts through the chaos. "Ange? What's going on?"

Fumbling, I work to get my flashlight out. The hole is about four or five feet across. Elliot's gut-wrenching cries erupt from below. "El?! El, are you okay?!" I shout. Dipping the flashlight in the ripped hole, the light dances in the space, but doesn't illuminate Elliot's position.

Jackson's voice crackles. "Talk to me. Ange."

"The floor boards gave," I reply. "He fell through to the basement."

"Is he okay?"

"He's hurt. Bad, I think."

There's silence on the other end. Jackson comes back on the line. "So, Mrs. Green says there isn't a basement. Are you sure he fell that far?"

"What do you mean there's no basement?" I shine my flashlight deeper into the hole. "He's in some sort of room. There are walls. A floor."

"Okay, okay."

The flashlight finally catches Elliot amidst collapsed wood beams. He holds his leg and groans in pain.

"Elliot, talk to me! Please," I call down to him.

He grimaces, rocking back and forth. "My ankle. I heard something pop. Holy hell it hurts."

"You're going to be okay," I say. "We're going to get you out of there." My mind races. We're far away from a hospital, maybe a thirty or forty-minute drive, and the roads are slippery with rain. Power may be out. I try to conceal my panic as Elliot grunts, reaching for his camera.

He turns the camera on, pointing the lens at his injured ankle. Gingerly, he touches the swelling skin and lets out an agonized cry. "Don't think I can walk!"

"Just stay calm," I call out from above. "We're getting help!"

Down the hallway, I hear frantic footsteps. Jackson races around the corner. "Jesus," he says when he sees the hole in the floor. "How'd this happen?"

"It just…the whole thing gave."

Jackson carefully steps to the edge of the hole. "El!" he calls out. "You alive, man?!"

"Yeah! Think I need to go to the hospital though."

"We're going to get an ambulance, buddy! Just hang in there!"

"Okay!" Elliot replies, his voice faint.

"Did you call 9-1-1?" I ask.

"Beth is," Jackson replies. "What the hell were you doing here in the first place? Wandering off like that."

"I saw something. And it's not like we had a detailed map."

"We don't go off course. We talked about this," Jackson says. "Why don't you ever listen?"

"You mean why don't I do exactly what you say?"

"You're just like Mom. Stubborn." Jackson looks away. "You okay?" he asks.

"Just a little shaken up."

"He'll be fine. He's alive."

"You guys…" Elliot calls out to us. "*Guys.*"

"What?" Jackson says. Elliot pans the night vision camera across the floor. "You *need* to look at this!"

"What is it?" I ask.

"Just get down here. Now." Elliot's eyes widen like a deer trapped in headlights.

Jackson runs to get a ladder from the back of the Tahoe. Sliding my knees as far as they can go over the splintered wood, I perch myself at the edge of the gaping hole. The floor groans underneath me. I make sure to keep the light shining on Elliot.

"This is seriously messed up!" Elliot says.

"What? What are you seeing?"

"I…I don't even know!"

I tilt my head, hoping to hear Jackson running back to us. Soon, there's banging down the corridor. Metal on wood. Jackson comes rushing down the hall. I help him slide the ladder into the broken floor.

"El! Buddy," Jackson calls. "Watch yourself, all right? We're lowering a ladder."

Inch by inch, we lower the metal frame. It clangs as it hits the concrete floor. We try to secure the ladder against the rotting wood, but the wood is so old that it snaps under the weight. Finally, we find a sturdy enough section to rest the ladder on.

"You go first," Jackson says. "I'll hold it."

"No way," I reply.

"You're lighter," he says. "We have a better chance with you."

I hesitate, and then shimmy precariously onto the ladder. When I look back at Jackson he seems distracted. "You got it though, right?"

"What? You don't trust me?"

Throughout my life, Jackson has thrown out those little words to get me to do an array of stupid stuff. At this point, trust has nothing to do with it. I've been scraped and scratched and have fallen from so many random heights, I really don't want another scar. Plus, it's a long way down. I cock my head. "What about the maple tree behind East Hills?"

"I was *twelve*."

"My knee still clicks weird when I walk."

He stares at me like he doesn't have time for this. I relent and climb down into the darkness, the shadows engulfing me on all sides like a black sea. The ladder is slick with rain. My hands slide over the metal. It takes all I have to not lose my grip. Focusing on one rung at a time, my feet finally touch the ground.

The basement smells like rotting eggs, and something else I can't quite place. Copper? That dull ringing picks up in my ears. I wait for little girls to jump out at me, but when nothing happens, I pull out my flashlight and aim the light at Elliot. His ankle is red and bloated. I grimace, looking away.

"Tell me about it," Elliot says. I know my reaction isn't helping, so I try to keep a straight face.

Jackson peers down from above. "You got it down there?"

"Hang on," I say, holding the ladder. "Okay."

Jackson swings a leg over the edge. Elliot shifts his body, looking to the left. "Here," he says. "Shine your light over there…"

I sweep my flashlight across the floor, the walls, the ceiling. Bile rises in my throat. The room is definitely a holding cell of some kind. Strewn fetid mattresses line one corner, dried red and yellow stains splattering the cotton. Crude foam cutouts attach to the exposed overhead beams. On a couple of walls, fingernail scratches etch on the concrete.

As I hold the ladder, Jackson makes his way down. When his feet touch the floor, he freezes. For once, he can't think of anything to say. He picks up a mangled knot of leather straps and razor teeth off the ground.

"Is that a muzzle?" I ask.

He drops it and wipes his hands on his jeans, glancing at the only wall of the room with neat, paisley wallpaper. He raises his head, looking up to the ladder again.

"We need to get Beth," he says. "We need to get out of here."

I nod, though my gaze is fixed on the wallpapered wall. With all the rot around us, it seems strange that section of the room is so orderly. Walking closer, I inspect the delicate flowers on the paper, noticing one piece is frayed and creased.

I peel back the faded floral design to find a scribble carved into the cement. It takes me a second to realize the scribbles are letters, forming a small-four letter word:

h e l p

Studying the word on the wall, my mind blurs with the implications. Did one of the girls write this? How long were Herman's victims down here before he had his way with them?

I continue to peel the wallpaper, finding more and more etchings. *This isn't happening,* I think. *Please. This isn't happening.* A door has opened in my mind to a very dark place, and I want that door closed.

"Jackson," I say.

"What?" His back is to me as he tries to lift Elliot up. Elliot groans, trying to get his footing.

"*Jackson,*" I repeat. There must be something in the way I say his name, because he stops what he's doing and actually listens. Stepping back, I show him the bare wall. Words litter the space, the abandoned messages of Herman's victims...

HeLP   sAve Us   hElp uS   HeLp

The letters create a tapestry in front of us. Hundreds of desperate pleas stained with blood. The fear in this room expands, converging into a tangible entity. I see things, snippets of moments. I'm not sure if it's my imagination or if I've unlocked some portal into the past. A man stands in the doorway. A girl crouches in the corner. Fingernails on concrete. Screams in the night.

I look away, trying to regroup, but a picture in the middle of the wall brings me back to reality. It's a crude drawing of a child's face with an X covering her mouth. Where was Mrs. Green through all of this? Where were the police?

"Do you think we're the first?" I ask.

"The first what?" Jackson is numb beside me.

"To find this place. Since the murders. That's what they said in the newspapers. That they never found where he did it."

"Who else could have known?" he replies.

"She wanted us to find it."

Jackson turns to me. "Mrs. Green?"

"No. Tammy."

"What the hell is a Tammy?"

"The girl. That I saw. That Elliot and I were following."

Jackson lets out a groan. "We really doing this again?"

"I know it sounds nuts. But…ever since I've been off my meds."

Jackson rolls his eyes. "Come on, Ange. It's all in your head."

"It's *not*. I've been seeing stuff."

"I have to say, I'm disappointed. I thought you were stronger than this."

"Jackson, I'm not making this up!"

"She's not," Elliot says. He shifts under the weight of his damaged ankle. Jackson glares at Elliot. "The EMF meter was going off the charts. And it wasn't rigged. There's something here with us. And Angela saw it even before the meter picked up."

"The meter doesn't work. You were screwing with that thing the whole way here."

"I saw that girl, Jackson," I say. "And the other ones. Before Mrs. Green even showed me the photos."

Jackson waves his hand dismissively. "Probably saw them online. When you looked this place up. Just tricked yourself into thinking that."

"She led us right here. Tammy. She led us right to that spot in the floor," I reply. "It's not a coincidence that we ended up down here."

"Yeah. Thanks, Tammy. Bitch," Elliot says.

Jackson turns, placing a hand on the ladder. "Fine. Think whatever the hell you want."

"Where are you going?" I ask.

"I'm making sure Beth got a hold of someone."

"You're leaving Elliot down here?"

"You'll be here."

"But you're stronger than I am."

"So?"

"But what if we have to move Elliot?"

"He's not going anywhere," Jackson says. "Unless you think we're going to be attacked by some ghosts?"

"But say something happens? He's a sitting duck down here."

"A sitting duck for what?" Jackson asks.

"Just…you should stay. I'll go. I'm fast. Okay?" I say, ascending the ladder.

"Are you kidding me?" Jackson calls out.

"I'll be right back," I say, trying to hide the desperation in my voice. I don't want to explain to Jackson that everything about the dank, musty space makes my skin crawl. When I'm at the top of the ladder, he's still looking up at me, his face darkening, and for a split-second it almost seems like there's panic there too, like maybe he's just as frightened as me to be down there. I keep going, vanishing up through the floor before he can stop me.

8

It doesn't take long to reach the den, but when I do the room is empty. On the table, Beth's walkie lies on its side. The computer plays her fake sound effects on a loop, the whispering of little girls over and over again. I survey the room, listening deeply, but can't make out any other sounds except my feet on the hard wood floor. "Beth? Mrs. Green?"

I try to shut off the whispering loop, but the voices won't mute. Finally, I just pull the plug. In the silence, I breathe deeply, stepping back, and unexpectedly bump into Mrs. Green. She's carrying a glass of water and it slips from her hands, crashing on the floor. The glass shatters.

"Oh, dear," she says, her face flushed. Slowly, she bends down, her knees creaking, and picks up the pieces.

"I'm sorry," I say. "Let me." She stands over me awkwardly as I gather the glass shards. "Where's Beth?" I ask.

"Beth?" Mrs. Green says absent-mindedly.

"Yes, my partner. The one at the computer?"

"Oh." Mrs. Green looks around. "She was here a minute ago. I was bringing her some water."

"Okay…" I say. "And she called 9-1-1. Right?"

"9-1-1?"

"Yes. Elliot needs help. Did she call?"

"Oh no. Is your friend that hurt?"

I stare at Mrs. Green, my frustration mounting. "He fell through the floor," I reply.

Mrs. Green blinks at me. "Your friend will be back," she says. "I saw her with Manuel. Yes, I saw her with the phone. I remember now. I'm sure she called."

Mrs. Green's breathing is labored as she shuffles along. Something doesn't add up. Why would Beth not be in the room? She always does what Jackson says. If Jackson told her to stay in the den, she would have stayed in the den. So, where is she? I walk into the next room, calling out Beth's name, but no one answers.

Out the window, I see that Mrs. Green is now outside. She's talking to Manuel, who doesn't look too concerned. Mrs. Green sees me watching and smiles. She slowly trudges to the house. I step away from the window.

In the deserted kitchen I pick up the phone, clicking the receiver. Once. Twice. But there's no dial tone. I slam down the phone right as Mrs. Green appears in the doorway. "Manuel's still working, but he hasn't seen her. Maybe she stepped out?"

"Stepped out where?" I ask. "And the phone's dead. Are you sure you got through?"

Mrs. Green shakes her head. "Yes. We just called 9-1-1."

"Who just called? Beth? You didn't say that before."

"My dear, you're all red," Mrs. Green replies. "Do you want to sit down? Maybe Manuel can help."

With mounting frustration, I watch Mrs. Green totter to the back door again. She doesn't even look at me. "Manuel always knows what to do." She talks under her breath, her shaking hand fumbling with the door handle.

There's no time for this, I think. *No time.* With that familiar dread coursing through me, I turn away from Mrs. Green, taking off down the hall.

I'm breathing hard when I reach the hole to the basement. "You guys," I say. Jackson jumps to his feet.

"Where's Beth?" he asks.

"I can't find her. She's not in the den."

"What do you mean you can't *find* her?" Jackson springs to the ladder, climbing up rung by rung.

"Hold on," I say. "We can't leave Elliot. Hey. Stop."

"Did you call 9-1-1? Did anybody call?" Jackson asks.

"Green says Beth got through. But it was busted when I tried. Beth left her walkie…"

"That's weird," Elliot says. "Is Mrs. Green okay?"

"She's in the kitchen," I reply. "She's fine. Not helpful though. She's pretty out there."

"Are you sure the phone just died?" Jackson asks, still climbing.

"Yes. I know what I heard."

"So, Beth just vanished?" Elliot tries to move his leg, but winces under the weight.

"We can't leave Elliot down there," I say again.

"He's fine. We'll be back after we find Beth," Jackson replies.

"If there's someone else here…"

"You've really lost it, haven't you? Who would be here?"

He's about to step on the splintered wood, but I block him from climbing all the way up.

"We can't leave him," I say again.

Our eyes lock. Jackson doesn't move at first, but eventually he sighs. "Fine."

With both of us helping Elliot, we manage to pull him towards the top of the ladder. "Ow. Ow! Ow!" Elliot says.

"Sorry. Almost there," I say, hating how much pain he's in.

Jackson loses his balance, tilting backwards. The ladder wobbles and shifts. We push all our weight forward to stop from falling. My heart pounds against my chest.

"Careful," I say.

"I got it," Jackson replies. One of the metal ladder legs bounces, rocks, and rolls onto the other leg so we almost fall again. Elliot lets out another cry of pain. Jackson balances his weight, steadying the ladder. It settles on the basement floor. I reach up, and with Jackson's help, hoist Elliot onto the main floor above. He flops onto his back.

"Don't pass out on me," Jackson says, his face red. "We got to keep moving."

Elliot nods.

"You ready to stand?" I ask.

Jackson grabs him around the middle, propping him up. We stumble forward, rushing through the rooms. "Beth?!" Jackson calls.

"Mrs. Green?!" I call out. "Mrs. Green was going outside. She's probably outside," I say.

We walk through the living room, and Elliot weakens, dropping most of his weight on my shoulder. My knees buckle. "Sorry," he says. "Stepped on it wrong."

I lean him into a chair. "Here. Rest a bit," I say.

He grimaces. "Ow. Okay." I help him elevate his leg on a nearby chair. Jackson goes into the next room. I stay with Elliot, keeping him company. Every now and then he shudders in pain. "I'm sorry," I say. "Shouldn't have led you down that hall. I had no idea."

He catches his breath. Elliot studies me, his face somber. "I was serious back there. I do believe you."

"Yeah," I reply. "And now you can barely walk. Whatever this is. Whether I'm crazy or this is real. We're in over our heads."

Elliot tries to move his ankle, then grimaces. "You're really good about that, huh?"

"What?"

"Shutting people out."

"Better that than someone getting hurt," I reply. "You probably think I'm the biggest weirdo that ever was."

Elliot grins. "I've always thought you were a weirdo. It's what I always dug about you." Our eyes lock. I will myself not to look away, but then his eyes drift to the ground. "Hey. Look."

Tiny droplets of blood glisten on the floor. They lead to the back door. I call out Jackson's name and he comes running.

"What? What is it?" he asks.

When Jackson sees the blood, his face pales. He follows the splatter into the kitchen, and then to the door leading to the backyard. Wrapping my arms around Elliot, I help him stand, but Jackson's too focused on the blood to wait for us. He opens the kitchen door into the backyard and reels back.

A shadowed, hulking man blocks Jackson's path. I let out an involuntary yelp, but when the man steps into the light, it's Manuel. His jacket is soaked through.

"*Jesus*," Jackson says. After a moment, he recovers. "Beth. Have you seen her?" he asks Manuel. "Blonde? This high?"

In response, Manuel rattles off some Spanish. He glances around, wiping his face with his sleeve. I try to make out what he's saying. He seems distracted as he peers into cabinets and turns on the kitchen sink.

"What the hell is he saying?" Elliot asks.

"He's speaking too fast," I say.

Manuel wrings off his jacket, still muttering to himself.

"Screw this. Come on." Jackson shoves past Manuel and dashes through the rain.

"But maybe he can help," I say.

Elliot hoists himself up, clinging to the kitchen table for support. Slowly, he limps behind Jackson. With one last look to Manuel, I head out the back door. Even when the door slams shut, I can still feel Manuel's eyes on me.

In the rear courtyard, Jackson rushes through the vine-entwined space. He cups his hands to his mouth. "Beth?! Beeeeth!" he yells. Elliot teeters on the grass. I help him lean against the wall of the house.

In the middle of the lawn, Jackson's body tenses. His eyes fixate on the pond and he lets out this heart-wrenching cry. Hard rain pelts the murky, weed-encrusted surface.

"Oh no," Jackson says. "Oh no, oh no, oh no."

Floating in the middle of the swampy pond, a tangle of blonde hair bobs up and down. Jackson rushes towards that blonde hair at full force. "Beth!" he calls out. "Beth!" I follow him through the rain, splashing in puddles.

He reaches the edge of the pond and extends an arm over the murky water. His fingers grab a few strands, but then an odd expression crosses his face. He shuffles back, staring at the bobbing hair.

"What is it?" I ask. "Jackson?"

Kneeling down, I reach for the wispy blonde hair. My toes teeter at the edge of the pond. Rain pelting my face, I grab the hair and gently pull it towards me. The clump rolls over to reveal plastic eyes and a mouth that has been stitched shut.

Elliot cranes his neck from where we left him. "What is that? Is it Beth?" he says. His voice hardly carries over the rain.

"It's a doll," Jackson replies.

I reel my arm back, careful about how I shift my weight so I don't fall in. Dirt clings to my shoes as I slide over the grass. Suddenly, a child's hand pokes up from the liquid surface. Tiny mud-slick fingers graze my wrist.

I jump back, my ears ringing, and so does Jackson. His jaw drops as I stumble back onto the lawn. Catching my breath, I look back to the pond, but there's nothing there but the doll.

A small bead of blood trickles from Jackson's nose. He sniffs, wiping it away with his hand. Before I can say anything, he walks back towards the house. Did he see the girl too? The question sticks in my throat.

Thud!

Through the rain and wind, a banging comes from above. *Thud!* In the storm, it's a low sound, but distinct enough for all of us to look up. There's a figure in the top attic window. It's hard to see, but there's someone banging on the glass. *Thud! Thud!*

Jackson steps forward, transfixed. "Beth?"

The figure's just a dark shadow with long hair. Maybe it's not Beth, but who else would it be? Jackson takes off running. "Hang on!" he shouts.

"We don't even know if that's her," I call out to him. "It could be anyone."

"Anyone? Who else would it be?" Jackson asks. "These conspiracy theories have got to stop, Ange. Reality can't be changed. There are no loopholes. No *other side*."

"But how do you know?" Elliot asks.

Jackson throws up his hands. "Forget you both. I don't have *time* for this." He bounds back into the house, slamming the door behind him.

"We need to go after him," I say.

"I know," Elliot replies. He leans on me, his heart beating wildly against my chest. I help him through the door, sliding over the concrete.

Inside the house, I listen for movement as thunder rolls outside. We wind our way through the dark rooms. Lightning strikes, and the hallway is briefly illuminated. The photographs of the children seem menacing now, like they're watching our every move.

When we reach the base of the stairs, Elliot's out of breath. He grasps my hands tightly, trying to balance as we take it one step at a time. Above us, Jackson yells out Beth's name. By the time we reach the top step, Elliot's shivering. His ankle is a garish purple. We still need to make it up the heavy wooden ladder to the attic. Muffled moans erupt from above.

"Forget it," Elliot says, sweat clinging to his face. "Just slowing you down. Go on ahead."

"We can do this together."

"I'll wait for you here. You'll be coming down soon anyway." He smiles. "It'll save me the trip."

I nod and set him down by the rickety ladder. Climbing up into the darkness, I survey the vast, vaulted space. The attic runs almost half the house, though there are some spots that are too low to stand up straight. Cobwebs cling to strewn piles of junk.

"Jackson?" My voice barely rises above the storm.

A guttural moan emerges from the shadows. I freeze, trying to locate the voice. "Beth?" I gingerly cross the floor. By an abandoned rocking horse, I step in a wet, slick substance. "Jackson? Where are you?"

Faint moonlight spills into the attic from a lone window. Past a row of boxes, I spot Jackson. He hunches over a slim body tucked in the shadows. Beth. "You found her. Thank God," I say, but rushing closer I see that something is very much wrong.

Beth is huddled on the ground. Her clothes are smeared

with blood and she's groaning. I've never seen my brother so scared. "Ange. Help," he says, stroking Beth's hair.

"What happened?" I ask.

He shakes his head. "She won't show me her face. I found her like this. Come on, baby. You have to show us. We can't help you if you don't show us."

Beth sobs, her voice muffled. She tilts her face up. A shard of moonlight catches her skin. I stifle a scream. Gnarly black thread sews her lips shut. Beth moans, her eyes widening. I kneel beside her and place a hand on her shoulder.

"Oh, god," Jackson says. "Who did this? Who?"

Beth just whimpers. She claws at her lips, trying to pry them open. "Mmm! *Mmmm!*"

"Careful," I say. "Let us help you."

"Mmmm!"

My mind reels as Beth gags and convulses. The thread is thick and course, not easily broken. "Jackson, your pocket knife."

Jackson pulls out a Swiss Army knife. He extends the tiny scissors. "Hold still. Okay…hold still." Tears form in his eyes. He props the scissors up, closing in on the thread. She breathes fast through her nose. I hold her head, keeping her steady.

"Please, baby," Jackson says. "I'm trying to help you…"

She gurgles in response. He slips the blade under the first stitching. Tears flood down Beth's cheeks. *POP.*

Then the next stitching…*POP.* Beth grumbles in pain.

"It's okay. It's okay. Almost there," Jackson says.

POP…POP…

"Who did this? Who would do this?" I ask.

POP...

Blood begins to trickle through Beth's opening lips, dribbling down her chin. She trembles as Jackson maneuvers the scissors around the last stitching. *POP.*

"There it is. There we go," he says.

We help her sit upright. Beth opens her mouth, copious amounts of blood drool out. She coughs hard, gagging, and lets out a wretched cry.

"Okay," Jackson says, going into survival mode. "I'm going to get you out of here. We're getting out of here." He bends down and scoops Beth up like a child.

I hold the flashlight up, lighting Jackson's path as he rushes past the dusty boxes and down the attic steps. Elliot struggles to get out of Jackson's way. "What happened?" he says. "Beth?"

Jackson lays Beth on the ground. I rub her shaking arms as she stares at the wall. "Do you know who did this?" I ask. "Who did this to you?" Beth doesn't answer. She barely blinks.

Jackson strips off his t-shirt and tears it down the middle. Using it as gauze, he gently stuffs it into Beth's mouth. "Shh," he says. "This'll stop some of the bleeding."

"We need to get the car and get the hell out of here," Elliot says.

"Agreed," Jackson says.

"Shouldn't we look for Mrs. Green? Tell her we're leaving?"

"You help him," Jackson says, ignoring my question. "I'll get Beth. Come on."

We all stagger down the stairs to the massive oak doors.

I yank the handle. *Oh no.* The handle's locked. The door won't open.

"What's wrong with you? Push!" Jackson says.

"I am," I reply. "It's stuck or something."

Jackson looks from me to the door and back to me again. "Push harder," he says. When I do and nothing happens, he lets out a frustrated cry. He sits Beth in a chair and she pulls her knees to her chest.

Jackson tries the door, but it won't budge. "What the…?" He struggles with the lock, pushing into it with all his weight. When that doesn't work, he pounds on the door, throwing his shoulder into it. He kicks the wood. "Through the kitchen," he says, picking Beth up and carrying her in his arms once again.

In the kitchen, we head straight towards a set of swinging doors that lead to the adjoining hallway. I push open the doors, but they only open halfway before *whamming* shut again.

Lurching back, I exchange a startled look with the others. "You've got to be kidding me," Jackson says. He leans into the doors, using all his weight, but the doors won't budge. "Come on," he says, looking my way. "Help me. Push."

I tilt my shoulder into the door, digging my heels into the ground. Jackson shakes his head, trying to put together the pieces. "How'd that happen?" he asks. "How'd they just close? You were looking, right? You saw that? No one was on the other side. How'd they close?"

He rears back and kicks the door. *Clomp!* The door sticks. "Back hallway," Jackson says.

"Wait," Elliot says. He reaches toward the counter and fumbles to pull a carving knife out of the chopping block.

"Good call," Jackson says.

Together, we turn down the narrow hallway to the back door. I can't help feeling, as we stumble towards any sort of escape, that the house is patiently waiting for us to fail.

Jackson looks back to me. "We're going to find a way out of here, sis," he says firmly. "We're all getting out of here."

The steady pattering of rain and Beth's frail, shaky whimpers cut through the darkness. We reach the back door, and I twist the handle, but it's locked. Unlatching the deadbolt, I try again. The door won't budge. "Something's forcing it shut," I say.

"Not possible," Jackson replies. "Move."

He pounds on the door with his fists, ramming his shoulder into it. Then he kicks and shoves the wood. With growing dread, I watch my brother try, again and again, to make this right. My mind races. Why is this happening? Why is this happening?

"They're trying to keep us here," I blurt out.

Jackson picks up a heavy, iron coat rack. He furrows his brow. "What are you talking about?"

"The girls. They don't want us to leave. I think they might have Mrs. Green."

Jackson growls and continues working on the door. "I'm done listening to your crazy theories, Ange!"

"You see them too. Out in the courtyard. That hand in the water. I know you saw it. Don't lie to me. I know." Jackson glares at me, still trying to pry open the door. "And you've seen them before," I continue. "You drink and smoke, trying to ignore the fact that we're both becoming just like her. But you can't. You can't hide."

Jackson stews. I think he might lash out, maybe punch me, or wrestle me to the floor, but he only stands there, trembling, lost in his own thoughts.

"How long, Jackson?" I ask. "How long have you been seeing them?"

He glances away, then studies me head on, his glassy eyes cutting right to my core.

"Just help me get out of here." Jackson says. "Please?"

The kitchen clock ticks and tocks above our heads. Beth whimpers in the chair. Elliot puts a hand on her shoulder, trying to calm her down. I throw off the jackets on the coat rack, nodding to my brother.

Jackson stands on one side and I stand on the other. We lift the rack and smash the dense iron base into the door.

WHAM! WHAM! WHAM!

The wood starts to splinter. "Keep going," Jackson says.

WHAM! WHAM!

The frayed edges grow, bending and breaking, until there's a satisfying crack. The door collapses in front of us. Jackson shoots me a victorious look as he throws the coat rack down.

Jackson cradles Beth through the doorway. The rain greets us in full force. I hold on to Elliot, propping him up in the slick grass. We snake around the house, making our way through the sheets of rain. I force myself to not look back at the pond with the drowned doll or the dark windows where little girls may be watching.

"We're almost there!" Jackson calls out. He looks over his shoulder to make sure Elliot and I are still behind him.

Reaching the front of the house, we trek through the mud towards Jackson's Tahoe.

"Come on," Jackson says. "Let's *go*."

My ankle twists on a soggy lump of grass. When I look down I notice it's not grass, but the ratty old teddy bear Claire was holding in the house. Swiveling around, I scan the lawn ornaments and shrubs. Is she watching us now? Are they all watching us?

"Get moving, Ange," Jackson says. He tucks Beth into the passenger seat. She limply falls back and stares at the dashboard. "Okay. Baby. Here we go. We're getting you out of here."

Jackson opens the door for Elliot. We both help him lean into the back seat. I climb in beside Elliot and buckle him and myself in. Jumping into the driver's seat, Jackson strums his hands on the wheel. He's about to turn the key in the ignition when he looks in the rear view mirror and curses.

Behind us, the massive iron gate is closed. I share a worried look with Jackson.

"Lock the doors," he says.

"Where're you going?" Elliot asks, but Jackson's already slamming the driver's side door shut. He takes off for the gate. I press down on the manual locks. Elliot does the same. The three of us sit in silence. Rain pelts down on the hood.

Jackson sprints through the mud, arms pumping and legs churning. He scrambles to the gate and tries to push it open. *Clank-Clank-Clank.*

Jackson shoves the gate. He steps back, surveying the metal. Fear engulfs me. Whoever stitched Beth's lips shut could still be here. Jackson's not safe. No one is. I think about

Mrs. Green. Where the hell did she go? Does that monster have her? Maybe it's Manuel. Maybe he did it. Unless it's someone else entirely.

Elliot tries to swivel around. "Did he get it?" he asks.

I shake my head. "Not yet."

Jackson sprints back in our direction. "Here he comes," I say, unlocking the driver's door. Jackson climbs into the car, soaked to the bone.

"We're stuck here? Aren't we?" I say.

"No." Jackson says. He shivers, his teeth chattering.

"The gate's locked," I reply.

"I'm handling it." Jackson jams the key into the ignition. "Please work," he says under his breath. "Please work." He cranks the key. The starter catches and the engine turns over. The car rumbles to life. "First try! Yes! Thank you. Let's do this."

"Do what?" Elliot says. My brother gives me a steely gaze in the rear view mirror. Jackson drops the car into drive and mashes the pedal.

"Wait." My stomach lurches. "You're not going to…" The tires kick up mud, the wheels catching and groaning. The old truck fishtails down the driveway.

He's going to ram it, I think. *He's going to ram the gate.* We race toward freedom. The speedometer climbing.

25…30…

"We'll get through," Jackson says.

"What if we don't?" I say.

"We'll get through!" Jackson barrels straight for the exit. 35…40…

"Oh, Jesus," Elliot says.

45…50…

Jackson grips the wheel, eyes filled with determination. Faster. Faster.

55…60…

The gate's coming up quick now. We're almost there. We're *almost* there. Jackson gives a little whoop. "Let's do this," he says. "Let's. Do. This."

His foot crushes the gas.

Elliot holds my hand tightly. I smile, scared out of my mind. The car headlights illuminate metal. I brace for impact.

And that's when Claire steps into view.

Ringing erupts in my ears. She stands in the middle of the driveway, her gaze stoic, her hands covering her mouth.

"Jackson, no!" I say.

Jackson startles, his eyes widening like he sees Claire too. He steels himself and floors it, hitting Claire head on. The car passes through her. Jackson raises his fist and hollers at the night, until, that is, Manuel's shocked face appears out of nowhere.

Balking, Jackson turns the wheel.

Manuel's hands go up in meek defense. The car knocks him down.

There's a crunch, the tires rolling over him. We lose control on the bump. The car lurches, tires skidding through puddles and mud.

The rubber kicks up rocks and grass. We spin out of control. I hold on to what I can. Elliot jams his ankle, letting out a harrowing cry. Even Beth startles awake.

"We're okay. We're okay. We're okay," Jackson says, desperately trying to regain control of the car.

The headlights ignite a massive oak tree in front of us. We're barreling straight for it. It grows larger in the windshield.

Before I can blink, metal collides with bark. WHAM!!! The hood accordions. The car's frame twists. Glass shatters, slicing past my face. Jackson's seatbelt catches. He jerks forward, hitting his head on the wheel with a clunk. I'm tossed sideways with Elliot.

But Beth ejects from the passenger seat. She rockets through the windshield. The sickening crunch of bone pierces through the rain.

Everything stops.

Silence.

The rain hammers down. Smoke curls from the crumpled hood. I try to speak, but my voice sounds muddled, like I'm underwater.

"El," I say, swallowing hard. My ears no longer ring, but my head throbs. Elliot catches his breath, slowly checking his arms and legs to make sure he's still intact.

"Ange…" he says hoarsely.

Up front, Jackson slumps against the wheel, shrouded in a wisp of smoke. Blood trickles down his forehead. The windshield is a gaping hole of shattered glass. The reality of what just happened hits me full force. "Beth…Oh, God."

I try to move, but my leg is pinned behind the seat. It won't budge no matter how hard I tug. "Jackson, wake up," I say. A soft breath escapes his lips as I nudge him. Slowly, he sits up.

"You're bleeding," I say.

He touches his head, groaning. His eyes drift beside him.

"Where's…?" Jackson looks out the shattered windshield to the gnarled tree. "No," he whispers. He scrambles to undo his seatbelt. Opening the door, he falls out into the wet grass, still dizzy from the crash.

"Jackson, wait," I say. He lifts himself up. Limping, he makes his way to Beth. The rain hammers down. *We need to get out of here*, I think. *We need to find a way out.*

I look off across the massive yard, back up the driveway to the house.

On the steps I see something. A hulking figure three times as big as Mrs. Green stands in the rain. This figure is broad-shouldered. He gazes out at us, a cap hiding most of his face. Casually, the figure walks down the steps. Prowling across the lawn towards Jackson.

"He's not real," I whisper. "He can't be real."

Elliot looks up. "What? Who is it?" He swivels around, but his leg prevents him from turning all the way.

Outside the car Jackson doesn't notice the hulking figure. All he sees is Beth with her skull split open, her arms and legs shredded. "Baby?" he says. "Come on, baby."

I struggle to pry my leg free. Shards of metal dig into my flesh. Willing myself to be strong, I give my leg one hard tug. "Gnhaaaa…*shit*!"

Looking back out the window, I see the figure pick up a shovel by a clump of shrubs and move in on Jackson. He maneuvers the shovel so it's like a baseball bat in front of him. When he's ten feet away, I finally see the figure's face. My blood runs cold. I've seen that face before. It's the same as the mug shot I found online, only older. Beaten down.

Herman.

"Jackson!" I call at the top of my lungs. My mind reels. "*Jackson!*"

Herman's close enough now for Elliot to see him too. He goes into a full on panic and calls out Jackson's name, but Jackson's not listening. He's too busy scooping Beth's limp body into his arms.

"Wake up. Baby. Open your eyes. Come on, baby." Jackson cradles her. "I promise we'll get out of here. Then it's New York all the way. Big NYC. I promise. I promise."

I yank at my leg. In the mud, Jackson tries to wipe the blood from Beth's face. It streams from her skull like an endless spring. "No, no, no. Beth," he says. "Talk to me…"

Beth doesn't move. I'm convinced she's dead, but then her head jolts. Her neck strains. Suddenly, her eyes open. For just a moment, she's lucid.

Jackson startles. "Baby?"

She twitches. Once. Then again.

"Wait. Don't do that. Don't do that," Jackson says. Blood gobs out of her mouth as Beth seizes, flopping in Jackson's arms like a fish out of water. He holds her down, trying to stop what's happening.

"Jackson!" Elliot and I call out to him from the car.

Herman's closing in. Jackson's head is bowed, focusing on Beth's face. She twitches again, weakening, and then goes still in his arms.

Jackson lets out an anguished cry. He buries his head in her neck. Herman's strides grow longer.

"Get away from him!" I say, pounding on the window.

Herman raises the shovel over his head, the steel handle pointed to the sky.

"Buddy, look out!" Elliot yells.

But it's no use. *Thwap*! Herman drills Jackson in the skull. Jackson doesn't even have time to look up. He crumples, knocked out cold.

"No!" I cry, tugging frantically at my leg, but no matter how hard I strain, my foot won't budge. Helplessly, I watch as Herman pulls a wheelbarrow from the garden and drags Jackson by his feet, heaving him into the wheelbarrow. He begins rolling Jackson back up the driveway towards the house.

Wriggling, I pull on my leg. Elliot examines the upholstery of the car. "Ange, the seat," Elliot says. "Can you…? If you move it…"

I reach out my hand, now pockmarked with blood from the shattered glass. Bending forward, fingers splayed, I strain for the lever on the front seat. "It's too far," I say.

"Here. Maybe…" He shifts his body in the seat, wincing as he tries to move his ankle. "Ow, ow, ow. Hang on." He thrusts his arm out. "Aghhhh!"

Slick with blood, his fingers tease the lever. He grips the plastic, but then his hand slips. He tries again, finding a firmer grip and pulling hard. *Thwunk*. The seat shifts forward, freeing my leg. Aching pain shoots up my thigh. I hold my calf with my hands, trying to stop the searing sensation.

Elliot flops back, catching his breath and sucking in through his teeth. Finally free, I look up at the house. It looms over the yard like a dark beast. Elliot hands me the carving knife.

"Help your brother," he says. Trembling, I take the knife.

Elliot puts his bloody hand on mine. I know it's morbid, but it's actually kind of comforting. Meeting his gaze, he forces a weary smile. "You're a tough chick. Something else I've always dug about you."

I climb over the driver's seat, sliding out the open door. In the wet grass, rain cascades down. I hobble to my feet, but then a snarling black *thing* pushes into me. That beast of a German Shepherd.

It lunges and grabs my arm, wrenching me to the ground. The knife flops into the grass. The dog's canines sink deep in my arm. "Get off! Let go!" I flail, swatting at the dog's face. Turning my head away, I see the knife lying on the grass a few feet away.

The dog tugs me back as I strain to reach for the knife handle, fingers splayed. Growling, the dog wrestles my arm. The further I reach, the more I feel my arm being shredding.

"Come on. Come on." Eventually, I wrap my fingers around the handle. Gripping it tightly, I whip around and plunge the knife into the dog's throat. *I'm sorry*, I think. *I'm sorry.* The blade goes into the flesh with a *thwip*. I feel the dog's racing heartbeat. It yelps, whimpering, but still bares its teeth. *Thwip!* I stab again, disgusted that I'm hurting a living thing, and then panicked because I can't feel my arm. *Thwip! Thwip!*

The dog growls and lets out one final shriek before flopping into the dirt. It squirms, it's chest rising and falling steadily and then not at all. I drag myself to my feet, holding my injured arm. The wound is deep, but nothing's spurting, which I take as a good sign.

I scan the area. By the front gate, the body of Manuel

tangles in the dirt. His limbs bend in odd angles. The rain pummels down as I bend over, retching. Whatever the hell's going on, whatever happens, I need to make this right.

The front door of the house is open a few inches. I march forward with the knife in my hand. Mud splashes on my soaked-through jeans. The thought of what that creep's doing to Jackson forces me to keep going. Even through the rain, Herman's creased shoe marks puddle on the front steps.

Placing a hand on the door, I push it open, half-expecting Herman to jump out at me. My heart pounds in my chest. No matter how hard I breathe, I can't calm myself down. I wipe the rain from my eyes.

Once I'm inside the house though, the ringing returns in my ears. It is at once intense and echoing. There's no escaping the head-pounding assault. Shuddering, I take a deep breath, steeling myself. I move to the open foyer, cautiously pivoting my head. The ringing ebbs and flows, like waves crashing on a rocky shore. I peek into various rooms, gripping that knife, searching for Jackson, but each room I enter is empty of life.

The clock ticks. The rain pours. But there's nothing else.

Then, halfway into the living room the ringing spikes momentarily. A small shadow flits past the doorway. Claire? Or is it Tammy? Moving past the furniture, I follow the shadow down a hallway, hoping I'll have the courage to strike if Herman jumps out at me. *You will be brave,* I think. *You have no choice.*

It takes me a second to realize that this is the hallway that leads to the basement. I walk down dark corridors. The wood groans underneath my feet. As I round a corner, I come to the gaping hole in the floor.

Claire stands by the ladder. She turns towards me with her hands over her mouth, except there's something different about her eyes. They're calm. Determined. Slowly, she lowers her hands and places them by her sides.

I step back, swallowing hard. Her lips have been sewn shut, just like Beth's. Claire stares at me, that incessant ringing quaking in my brain. I fight the urge to run in the other direction as her small frame bends backwards, crab walking down the hole into Herman's world.

Heading to the ladder, I see Claire is now standing in the basement, looking up at me. When I don't move, she walks into the shadows. Knowing what I have to do doesn't make this any easier. If I want to save my brother, I don't have any other choice but to keep going.

I slide over the floor on my belly, and then swing one leg, and then the other, onto the ladder. At first my shoe slips, and I hang precariously over the edge. Once I find my footing again, I climb into the darkness one rung at a time. That putrid, rotting smell is the first thing that hits me, though now it's mixed with the sweetness of wet grass and mud.

When my feet touch the concrete floor, Claire appears beside me. She steps to a fetid mattress strung up on the wall and then ducks behind it. I follow her, pushing the mattress away from the wall. A small pitch-black corridor's hidden on the other side.

"Claire?" I whisper, my voice frayed. Wind rustles down the corridor. It seems deep and narrow. Without being able to see, I'll be exposed, unable to fight back.

Glancing around the small basement, I look for anything I can use as a weapon, but find something better: Elliot's night-vision camera. It lies on its side, forgotten from the earlier hustle to get up the ladder. I flip it on.

Holding it up to my eyes, the night vision mode illuminates the dark corridor in a green tint. I slip behind the mattress, trying to be quiet as I follow the grainy green outline of the narrow concrete walls. My shoes kick up dirt. I can make out the faint imprint of Herman's large work boots on the dusty ground.

Sweat slides down my forehead, tickling my skin. Each groaning pipe causes me to jump. My breath comes out in heavy, trembling gasps. *Calm down*, I think. *Calm down.*

Inching my way through the darkness, rusty squeaking erupts in the shadows. I slow down. Listening. SQUE-EAK. SQUE-EAK.

Tammy. It has to be Tammy. But where is she? I round a corner and the corridor tightens. I have to crouch to keep going. SQUE-EAK. I halt. Waiting. Holding my breath.

SQUE-EAK. Wherever she is, Tammy's getting closer.

I look behind me, and then from side to side, moving quicker now. One hand lightly traces the cold wall. Feeling the cool rock on my skin provides a small sense of security.

SQUE-EAK! This time the sound is right behind me. *Oh no.* I turn in a circle, searching the darkness, but I'm the only one here. My skin crawls. Then why does it not *feel* like I'm the only one here?

Cautious, I turn again. This time around, a mass engulfs the viewfinder. Shiny metal glares in the green light. Tammy's face is inches from mine – or what's left of it. Her jaw is gone and her tongue dangles from her mouth.

"Gnnaaaaaahhh," Tammy says.

The ringing spikes in my ears as I push back. Without thinking, I whirl and bolt. The only thing on my mind is getting the hell out of there. Twisting my foot in the darkness, I keep going, hobbling forward, wincing with each step. When I look behind me, Tammy is still following me. SQUE-EAK. SQUE-EAK.

I duck around corners. The corridors expand around me, forming an intricate maze underneath the house. After awhile, I've been running so long I've lost my way. I reason I must be far away from the house by now. Perhaps by the pond, or maybe the grove of trees behind the property?

Slipping through an arched doorway, I sink to the floor and pull my knees to my chest. Grabbing fistfuls of my hair, I steady myself, preparing for what's ahead. "It's okay," I whisper. "They can't hurt you. Only you can hurt you. Only you."

Sometimes, when I was little, I'd find my mother in the closet in this exact position, whispering to herself and pulling out her hair. I'd open the door, and beneath the coats and clothes my mother would be huddled on the floor, looking up at me with wide, open eyes. When this happened, I would always crawl into the closet with her and my mother would wrap her thin, cold arms around me. We'd pray together, "Lord, make me an instrument of your peace. Where there is hatred, let me sow love, where there is injury, pardon, where there is doubt, faith, where there is despair, hope…" We'd repeat the prayer, over and over, our voices colliding, the dangers of this world and the next crashing towards us.

I imagine my mother's arms around me now, and I can almost feel them. "Where there is darkness, light," I whisper. In the silence, my voice sounds dangerous, a trespass. Years of quiet have woven into the walls and soaked into the soil. The hush is now an entity onto itself. I think of my brother, how he's down here with that monster, that *killer*. Struggling to my feet, I scan the darkness with the night vision camera.

I'm in a large room with a low ceiling. With the green light, it's hard to make out what's around me, but I'm surrounded by rectangular shapes that seem to be boxes. I step forward. My foot crunches down on a tangle of hard, lumpy sticks.

Leaning down, I investigate the small pile. I realize there are mounds of sticks around me, and that the whole room is full of them. Sticks on the walls, hanging from the ceiling like wind chimes, sticks on the floor forming little camps of clutter.

But that doesn't make sense. Why go to the trouble to construct these little tangles? *Maybe*, I think, dread slowly coursing through me, *because they aren't sticks at all*. I take another look at the pile by my foot and find a tiny skull.

"Oh, god."

Bones. They're *bones*.

I spin around, on high alert. There's a bucket of slop in the corner, a soiled mattress. Is this where he sleeps? Herman? Am I in some sort of secret room? Melted candles and faded photographs of the girls are propped in one corner.

Walking a few tentative steps forward, I notice there's another display tucked in the back of the room. I tell myself not to go ahead, but something pulls me closer. An instinct *beyond* the corridors of my mind, like an otherworldly whisper I can't ignore.

Look, the whisper calls. *Over here. Look at what he's done.*

I try to make out the lumps in the viewfinder. At first I think it's those girls again, but then I realize that whatever is here isn't moving and is just *clothed* in little girls' dresses. The green viewfinder light paints everything in a ghostly glow. I have to stand a few feet away to see that the dresses are adorned on crudely constructed girl-sized dolls. Tied and glued together animal and human bones form their delicate limbs, and each bone doll's tiny jaw is missing.

Bastard, I think. Anger fills me like a poison. Herman knew no one could hear those little girls scream. He knew no one could save them, because no one knew they were here. He stole them away in the night. He silenced them.

I lean over, my hands on my knees. From somewhere deep in the tunnels, Jackson cries out. I startle, taking in a deep intake of breath. Backing up slowly, I wave the night vision camera, searching for the arched doorway. I've never heard Jackson cry out like that. His voice echoes through the corridors. It cuts right through me. What is that monster doing to my brother?

In my panic to escape, my fingers slip from the night vision camera and it drops, clunking to the floor. For a moment, all I see is black. If there were ever a time *not* to freak out, this would be it, but with each cry from Jackson, I feel reality slipping away.

I fumble around the basement, past the delicate bones and junk. "Where are you?" I whisper. "Come on." I crawl, on my hands and knees, pushing past wet *things*. My heart beat races. I pray to find the camera. There's no way out without it. There's no way out.

My hands slide into sleek, foul smelling substances. Are those girls watching me now? Those sad, little girls. Around me, bones move, tangling towards me. Those little girls surround me, their laughter rising. *No escape. No escape.*

I feel that I'm on the edge of a giant precipice, about to fall. But then a miracle happens, something I'd never expect. My eyes…adjust.

There are no little girls here. Just bones and chairs draped in blankets, lampshades and buckets of slop. I don't need the camera. I never needed the camera. Jackson's cries echo down the corridor. I look to the left and see the faint outline of the arched doorway.

I'm coming for you, I think. *I'm going to save you.* I duck through the doorway. Stumbling forward, Jackson's screams become louder. I run through the darkness, following his cries. Pushing myself to hurry, I round a corner full speed, only to hit a cinder block wall. Dead end.

"No!" I slam my fist into the rock. My fingers make a cracking sound, but don't break. Backing up, I retrace my steps. Did I miss a turn? I went left before, but following the wall, I see there's another narrow hallway to the right. Adrenaline courses through me as I plow on.

Jackson. This way. Find him. Go.

Words fill my mind, but I'm not sure if I'm thinking them, or something else is intervening. A voice from the beyond? Maybe it's a higher power. An intuition I've long ignored.

I run as fast as I can without making a sound. At the end

of the hall I see a faint light raking across the concrete floor. Cautiously, I press against the wall, inching my way to the edge of an open doorway.

On the other side, the room tapers, stretching around a corner. There's a single lamp on a dirt floor. It's nice, with a beige shade that's slightly crooked. With a deep breath, I enter the room, scanning dark corners. It's only when I'm halfway inside that I spot Jackson. He's tied to a splintering chair, his head drooped to his shoulder. A rag is jammed in his mouth.

I stop cold. "Jackson?" I go to him, rushing to undo his bindings. It takes a second or two for his eyelids to flutter. He blinks awake, trying to raise his head. There are bloody bruises on his arms and legs. I dig my fingernails into the tightly bound knots, trying to loosen them. Jackson slowly comes to life. He shakes his head, his eyes widening. "Gahhh," he says. "Gahhh!!!!"

I pull harder on the bindings. "Shh. I'm going to get you out of here."

A shadow flits behind me. Claire? Before I can react, a hand shoves a rag over my mouth. Sweet, putrid chemicals fill my nostrils. I try to swivel around, but my attacker is strong. Leaning forward, I catch a glimpse of Herman's face. He leers down at me, his eyes cold. I feel myself slipping. I dig my nails into Herman's arm, but he presses the rag harder over her mouth.

The ringing crashes in my ears as I begin to lose consciousness. Behind Herman's shoulder, I sees Claire in the corner, watching. Quiet. Dots form in my eyes, my head swimming, and then everything goes black.

9

The first thing I notice is the smell of rubber, then mud and a sweet chemical taste in the back of my throat. A rough hand grasps my chin, pressing me back. Groggy, I open my eyes to find Herman duct-taping my forehead to a chair. Some of the hair by my temples rips out, causing pricks of pain in my skull.

I glance around, my vision blurring, trying to remember where I am. It's only when I see Jackson duct-taped to the chair next to me that it all comes back. I look to Herman, who stands off to the side. "What are you going to do to us?" I ask him. "Hey! What are you going to do?" He doesn't meet my gaze.

Blinking, the room comes into focus and I realize there's someone else with us. A hunched body stands by a small table, face bent over a tray lined with an assortment of instruments. At first, I think it's one of the girls, but then I realize it's Mrs. Green.

She's working away at something, her hands busy. The sound of metal clinks together. She lifts a scalpel, examining it in the low light.

"You're alive," I say, my brain still fuzzy. If Mrs. Green hears me, she doesn't respond. Jackson jerks his shoulders, trying to free himself. I follow suit, but the duct tape creases around my joints. I kick my feet, lift my knees, but Herman's strapped me down tightly.

Mrs. Green turns, smiling at us like a cheery grandmother. "Rise and shine, little birdies," she says. She walks to Jackson. Without warning, she pulls the rag from his mouth. He coughs, spitting on the ground.

"What the hell?! What is this?" Jackson strains his neck, trying to move his head. Mrs. Green holds him in place, parting his lips and prodding with her wrinkled fingers. She shushes him. "It's quiet time now."

Herman hovers over Jackson, who continues to wriggle, trying to wrench himself loose. "Hang in there, Jackson," I say, but this only elicits a long, sideways glance from Mrs. Green. It's at once predatory and pitying, a look I've never seen before from someone so old.

She smiles at Herman. As if on cue, Herman steps next to me. His eyes never leave Mrs. Green. I see his face clearly for the first time. There are ragged scars on his chin, pockmarked burns on his neck.

At the small table, Mrs. Green peruses the archaic instruments. Surgical blades. A chisel. A hacksaw. All the tools are stained with rust and God knows what else. Mrs. Green commands the room. There's a bounce in her step.

A fierce methodology to her actions. Her eyes gleam as she selects a pair of forceps and a set of surgical scissors.

"Should have known," she says. "A boy like you. Greedy. Just like my Herman. You need to learn. He learned. What he did to Claire…I'll never forget. And you…" Mrs. Green turns to me, a look of distrust on her face. "I wanted to stop them, but…I had no idea. That they could show you this. That you could hear."

I get an up close view of Mrs. Green's gnarled scar under the fluorescent bulb. "Good thing Mother taught me well," Mrs. Green says. "She'd use the belt. The gardening sheers. Burned my privates."

Jackson thrashes, trying to break free.

"It was the only way. I understand now. How the crying can drive a woman mad." Mrs. Green grips Jackson's jaw with her fingers, moving the forceps towards his mouth. He clenches his teeth shut.

She pushes on Jackson's lips. When his jaw won't budge, she pinches his nose. Jackson holds his breath. His face turns red and then blue as he jerks and twitches.

When he finally gasps for air, Mrs. Green jams the forceps between his teeth. "If those girls had only listened. Though maybe it was too much to ask. The way he ruined Claire. The way she screamed."

Mrs. Green grips the tip of Jackson's tongue with the forceps. He cries out. "Nah. *Gnahhh!*"

She lifts the scissors to his tongue. "You'd have to tell someone," Mrs. Green says, a deep ache in her voice. I try to put together the pieces, but everything's happening so fast.

Mrs. Green knew all along. She was the one that caused this pain.

"Why are you doing this?" I say. "Why?"

"Do you think I *want* this?" Mrs. Green asks. "Do you think I wanted to hurt them? I did what I had to do."

I glance at Herman, who stands in the shadows. Mrs. Green squeezes Jackson's tongue. "Nah! *NAHHHHHH!!!!*" He thrashes, drool dribbling down his chin.

Mrs. Green's shoulders hunch. She wipes her wet, saggy eyelids. "All I wanted," she says, "was a quiet house."

"Gnahhh," Jackson replies, staring at those scissors.

Mrs. Green moves away from him. She shakes her head. "But now you've found my little secret. My little boy. He's made such a mess of things."

Mrs. Green lifts her head, her expression hardening. She raises the scissors back to Jackson's tongue.

"No!" I shout.

Jackson howls and then coughs. Blood splatters the floor. I swallow back the vomit rising in my throat. Mrs. Green picks up the chisel. The hammer. Jackson squirms.

"Shhhh," Mrs. Green says. She wades over to him. "Hold still now…"

The veins in Jackson's neck bulge as he tries to break away.

"Please," I say. "Stop!"

"Shhh." Mrs. Green taps Jackson's chin. "This part's tricky. I'd hate to muck it up." She aligns the chisel with Jackson's jaw joint, just below his ear. He thrashes as she raises the hammer.

"*No!*" I scream.

THWACK. Chisel into bone.

Again. *THWACK.* And again.

Jackson screams. He makes low guttural sounds. I tear my eyes away from my brother. His flesh is now white. Twisting my arms, I manage to loosen the tape a little. Blood falls over Jackson's chair.

Mrs. Green moves back to Jackson with a needle and thread. He tries to shake his head, to keep her away, but she brings the needle to Jackson's lips and pricks the skin. Slowly, she sews his lopsided mouth shut.

"Shhh. It'll all be over soon," she coos. The needle weaves in and out. Blood drips down his lips. "Those girls. You have no idea," Mrs. Green mutters. "I told them families have secrets. But they lied to my face. Thought I couldn't hear the whispers. When the police came, I was ready. Herman was so easy to hide. So quiet. And Claire's body, what he had left, so small."

Herman stands in the corner, still as a statue. A flicker of emotion dances behind his eyes. Rage? It's hard to tell in this light. I look to my brother's broken face. His hazy eyes find mine.

"I'm so sorry…" I say. "I'm sorry I couldn't help you."

Jackson groans, the life draining out of him. *My fault. This is my fault,* I think. Jackson shakes his limp head. He's looking past me now, across the room.

At the edge of the darkness, buried in the shadows, Claire appears, followed by Tammy and Missy. All three of them stand together, side by side, though they're no longer covering their mouths. I see Tammy's missing jaw and dangling tongue, Claire's lips sewn completely shut, and Missy, with a red rubber ball jammed into her mouth and one long rusty nail skewering both cheeks.

The three girls stare at Jackson and me, and we stare right back at them. I look at my brother in awe. "You do see them," I say.

Jackson groans. He nods. *This is our own family secret. Our curse*, I think. Tears form in Jackson's eyes. He hangs his head, weighed down by regret. He's hidden it all this time. All that partying. All those drugs. They were distractions, ways to help him forget.

Mrs. Green glares at Jackson. "My goodness, young man. You sure do have a lot to say. Thought we had fixed that." She picks up a long, sharp whittle and marches towards him.

"Wait…don't!" I say.

"Don't worry," Mrs. Green replies with a smile. "You're next."

She raises the whittle. Jackson's too weak to respond. He gives me one fleeting glimpse before Mrs. Green moves between us, slamming the whittle down.

"Noooo!" I scream.

Jackson's entire body tenses. I strain against the tape as my brother begins to spasm. His limbs jerk like a broken marionette. The wooden chair bounces on the concrete.

Mrs. Green drops the whittle. It makes a crisp *thwick* sound as it hits the ground. She nods to Herman and he moves forward, untying Jackson by slicing the tape with a small knife. Jackson crumples to the floor.

"Leave him alone," I say, my voice wavering. "You crazy psycho, I swear to God. You leave my brother alone."

But Mrs. Green just cocks her head. "Oh my," she says. "Such language. We'll fix that right up. Won't we?"

I watch as Herman drags Jackson out of the room. Mrs. Green threads the needle again. She comes closer, pressing a wrinkled hand against my forehead. It's cold and wet from Jackson's blood. I squirm from the pressure of her hand on my skin.

Herman reenters, but Jackson isn't with him. As soon as I see him, I break down. "What did you do to him?" I say. A sob escapes my lips. "What did you do?!"

I think of all the times my brother told me to be quiet, how he always said what I saw was all in my head. Knowing now that he was there with me, willing himself not to believe that our mother was right all this time...

I look to the ghost girls. "Please. *Help*. Claire. Tammy. Missy." The girls don't move, though Claire tilts her head.

A curious expression crosses Mrs. Green's face. "Are they here?" she asks. Her nostrils flare. "What are they saying? What *secrets* are they telling you?"

"Please..." I say. "We'll never tell anyone. I promise. Just let us go."

With wide eyes Mrs. Green studies the corner, scanning the walls and the dirt floor. She seems lost in a distant memory, the past unfolding before her. "And Claire? My Claire, is she here?"

I don't answer Mrs. Green at first. The reality that my curse could give me some leverage is a small victory.

"You answer me, girl," Mrs. Green says. She places the sharp end of the scissors against my cheek. The pain is succinct and piercing. "Is she here?" Mrs. Green asks again.

Tears wet my face. The girls stand silently, but something's happening in the shadows behind them. Something's stirring from the darkness. Four more pale faces appear, all little girls. They drift into the light, joining the others.

"Oh, God," I say. "They're all here."

Mrs. Green blinks. "All…of them?" She falters, studying the corner. I'm amazed how my words affect her. She slouches, her eyes scanning the walls. The fact that she can't see them and I *do* unnerves her in a way I never would have expected.

"Where?" Mrs. Green says. "Where are my girls? I think you're lying. What do you see? Tell me what you see." She pushes the scissors harder into my cheek. A small bead of blood drips down my chin.

"There are seven of them," I say. "They're…disfigured. Some have stitched lips. Shattered jaws. Missing tongues. Teeth." I close my eyes, trying to get away from their sad stares. "They're looking at you and only you," I say.

Mrs. Green backs away from me, stumbling to the corner. I breathe deeply from this small respite, but it doesn't last long. Soon, I feel other eyes on me.

Herman. He looks me up and down, as if assessing my flesh. I'm not sure what sick things he's thinking, but I never want to find out. His towering frame comes closer and then slips behind my chair. I strain to see what he's doing, but can't move my head very far. *Oh, God. Oh, God. What is he doing?* I feel the bindings loosening.

Before Herman can get all the tape off, Mrs. Green whirls around. "*Wretch*," she hisses. "You'd betray the woman who protected you? And for what? A pretty face?"

Herman slowly moves away from my chair. It churns my stomach to think of what he's capable of, and what he would do to me if Mrs. Green weren't here. "Please," I say. "I can be useful to you. You want them gone? You want peace? I can help them go away. I can talk to them."

My words only seem to anger Mrs. Green more. She marches over and sticks the needle into my upper lip. It's a sudden movement, the pain sharp and stinging. A wave of fear rushes through me.

"Help! Somebody!" I cry. "Please!"

Mrs. Green smiles at me. "No one can hear you down here. I made sure of that. My little girls can't help you."

The long needle slides through my flesh, piercing my bottom lip. Mrs. Green caresses my cheek softly, looking furtively in the corner. "And are they watching us now?" Mrs. Green asks. "Ask them who called the wolves to my door. To take my Herman. Disappointments. All of them. They needed to learn."

She pierces my upper lip again with the needle. I cry out.

"Shh. Shhhhh," Mrs. Green says.

The corner of my mouth is now stitched shut. My mind drifts to Elliot. Maybe he managed to get over the fence. Maybe he's far from here now. I think of the unfairness of the world, that monsters get to live while innocents die. I convince myself I'm ready for this. Maybe in death I'll see my mother again.

Remembering my mother now, I can almost hear the words she repeated so many times: "We must let the light work through us, Ange. Where there is hatred, we must sow love. Where there is doubt, faith. Where there is despair, hope…"

Hope.

Out of the corner of my eye, there's a flicker of something. Someone. Elliot.

He's behind Mrs. Green and Herman, limping along the wall. He looks soaked and weak as he balances on one leg, but he's quiet. An involuntary moan escapes my lips, a cry of joy or pain or both. I do all I can to keep Mrs. Green and Herman's attention, making sounds, scratching the chair back and forth on the floor. Anything to keep alive what little hope there is.

Elliot picks up Mrs. Green's discarded cane on the floor. He staggers towards her as she threads the needle back through my lower lip. I flinch, no longer able to move the left side of my mouth. Elliot cautiously drags his busted leg. He hobbles along, almost to Herman. Raising the cane, he's about to strike, but then his foot catches on something. Oh, God. What is it?

The bloody whittle. It clink-clinks on the floor.

Herman turns. His mouth opens in a snarl when he sees Elliot. There's a wiggly little stump where Herman's tongue used to be. He lunges at Elliot, and Elliot swings the cane frantically, putting his full weight behind it.

The steel handle connects with Herman's face. He stands there stunned as Elliot swings again. *Crack!*

And again. *Crack!* The third blow catches Herman off guard. He flops sideways, knocking Mrs. Green's tray of tools over. Elliot's no match for Herman, who is bigger than Elliot and has two strong feet to stand on.

Growling, Herman swats at Elliot, coming at him with full force, but then the unexpected happens. Herman *trips.*

Elliot lays into him one more time, and though it's not a hard hit, it's enough for Herman to lose his balance.

He falls, his limbs flailing, and when Herman hits the ground he lets out a sudden sigh. Blood blossoms on his shirt like a bright red flower. The jagged end of a pipe peeks through his chest.

"What have you done? What have you done?" Mrs. Green rushes to Herman and holds his face tenderly with both hands.

With Mrs. Green distracted, Elliot uses the cane to hobble towards me and start breaking apart the tape restraints. *Hurry, hurry, hurry,* I think. Behind Elliot, Herman's breathing becomes more labored. I look over Elliot's shoulder, but can't fully see what's happening. Straining against the tape, I see that Herman stares into space, no longer breathing, and Mrs. Green is now glaring at us with a hacksaw in a bony hand.

I scream through my half-stitched mouth. Elliot turns, but Mrs. Green swipes him with the hacksaw, catching his shoulder. He cries out, crumpling to the ground. Blood flows from his torn arm. There's a fury on Mrs. Green's face I haven't seen before. She kneels, rolling Elliot over.

I work the tape loose, but it's stuck together. Desperate, I glance at the girls in the corner. They stand there, watching. "Please," I say to the girls. "Do something. You can do something."

Mrs. Green straddles Elliot. She presses down on his swollen ankle. Elliot cries out. The weight of her holds Elliot in place. I shimmy out of the now loosened tape and tug at the remaining binding around my ankles.

Every cry of pain from Elliot jolts my system. Mrs. Green raises the saw over Elliot, bringing it down hard. Elliot lifts his hands to block the blow. *Thwack.* The saw slices through his finger.

"Agghhh! Aghhhh!" His cries echo through the room.

The ghostly girls watch as Mrs. Green slices the saw into Elliot's clavicle. He cries out and blood soaks his shirt. Tugging at my bindings, I turn to the girls. "I know you can hear me. You can help us. I know you can."

Mrs. Green raises the saw again. I cry out, feeling the moment slow down as Mrs. Green prepares to deliver the final blow. In the corner, Claire winds up, straining against her stitched lips. The black thread stretches. She opens her mouth, letting out an ear-shattering scream. It's the loudest sound I've ever heard. I wince, covering my ears. Mrs. Green drops her hands.

"Stop," she says, searching the room. "What is that? What are you doing?"

All the girls start to make low, guttural moans. Claire's stitches pop as her mouth opens wider. The screams grow. A medley of squeals and moans erupt from the corner.

Still on his back, Elliot watches Mrs. Green as decades of pent up repression bombard her. The old lady closes her eyes, writhing. "You filthy children. Quiet! QUIET!"

But the screams only grow louder, building to an unbearable fever pitch.

It's too much. Too much even for me. In their screams, I feel the pain buried in these girls, the longing, the lives they'll never experience. All those lost days rattle around in my brain.

Mrs. Green falls to her knees. Through clenched teeth, she mutters, "Quiet! Quiet!"

With frozen fingers, I finish freeing my leg and fall to the dirt floor. A few feet away, the whittle lies by a puddle of Jackson's blood.

I wrap my fingers around it, rising to my feet. Mrs. Green is still hunched over, consumed by the dizzying voices. Giving it all I have, I lunge towards her. Mrs. Green's eyes widen. She raises her arms, trying to defend herself, but I swing widely and drive the long pointy piece of steel right into Mrs. Green's ear.

Thwip.

Mrs. Green's body freezes. The girls' screams slowly fade as Mrs. Green sways, the light leaving her eyes. Blood trickles from her eardrums and pours from her nostrils. She tilts to one side, toppling, her body thumping on the floor.

The girls stare blankly. Then, they do something I never would have expected. They *giggle*. Some of them point at Mrs. Green's crumpled corpse, while others jump up and down. I watch them for a moment, horrified, and then grab a scalpel from the floor, cutting the stitching from my lips.

Rushing to Elliot, I press my hands over his clavicle, trying to stop the bleeding. He's unconscious, his lips blue. I cradle him in my arms, thinking how I can make this right.

"El," I say. "Please come back to me. Please."

Running my hand through Elliot's hair, I study the tips of his eyelashes and the shape of his chin, wanting to remember every detail when he's still warm in my arms.

He's barely breathing. I stroke his cheek and then press

my ear to his chest, trying to listen for a heartbeat. Under his rib cage, a low thump echoes, and then dulls. *Oh, no. Oh, no. Oh, no.* "Please come back," I whisper. "I can't do this without you."

I'm not sure how long I hold Elliot in the darkness, but after awhile I feel him stir. A small cough escapes his lips. Elliot's eyes drift open. He looks beyond me, unable to focus. I laugh, just happy that he's still here. We breathe each other in, and for a moment I'm lost in his embrace.

That is until I hear a muffled voice. "Ange. Ange!"

Jackson. He's alive. He's still fighting.

I pull away from Elliot, noticing Claire and the other girls are still in the room. I hope Claire won't notice me, but then our eyes meet. Elliot studies me wearily. He knows something's up, but can't see Claire shuffling towards me. I lean back on my haunches, realizing I've never taken the time to look one of these ghosts calmly in the eyes before. Claire corners me. There's nowhere else to go.

The little girl cocks her head to one side, imitating Mrs. Green's sideways stare. Slowly, she holds out her hand, pointing. I flinch. What the hell is she doing? What does she want with me? But then I see Claire's not pointing at me, but *beside* me.

I glance to the left and spot the rusty gate keys clumped on the floor. *She's trying to help me,* I think. Claire looks at me with the wide eyes of a little girl. Nothing more.

Cautiously, I take the keys. There's a long, heavy silence between us. "Thank you," I say.

Claire lets out a little giggle. She turns, scampering off into the darkness. The other girls follow in tow, vanishing from the room. I look at the keys in my hand and then back down to Elliot.

"Hang on, El," I say. "I'm going to get us all out of here."

•   •   •

I run, retracing my steps, trying to find the way out of the dark. Corridor after corridor, I hear my heavy, urgent breaths. From somewhere in the shadows, a water pipe leaks, the dripping mocking me in the silence. The only thought in my head is to find Jackson. He's still alive. He could still be alive.

"Jackson!" I call out.

Come on. Say something. Let me hear your voice. Reaching the arched doorway, I step tentatively forward and my shoe slides into a slushy liquid that wasn't there before. I fumble forward, knowing I'm tired and not thinking straight. My body strains under the weight of all that's happened.

"Jackson! Where are you?" I yell. A plea this time, hoping he'll answer me. What good are the powers to communicate with the dead if I can't help the people I love?

My feet step on crunching bones, and there's a new smell. Rot and urine, mixed with the metallic whiff of blood. *Please, Jackson. Don't leave me. Please say something. Please.* But it's so dark.

So quiet.

Something's coming. Something's coming.

Panic tickles my throat as I hear that otherworldly voice again. I struggle to breathe as I think of those girls and the things he did to them. Monster. I can feel them pulling me, trying to reach out, to scream.

"Jackson..." Tears stream down my face. There's no end

to the darkness. I can see what Mrs. Green did to them. I can see how they cried. They're coming for me. Their hands brush my skin and try to pull me to the other side.

But I can't help them anymore. I have to find my brother. I'm no good for him here, blind and bleeding. "I'm going to get help. Okay? I'm going to help you," I sputter, backing up, hating myself for it. The hands brush into me as I feel my way to the arched doorway.

Out into the main room of the dungeon, I run. Sprinting past the old mattresses, the slick stains on the floor, up the rickety ladder. My hands tremble. The voices whisper behind me. *Come back. Come back.*

I will, I think. *I won't leave you.*

I barrel across the foyer towards the front door. If I had only known then what I know now…

But it's too late.

Outside, the rain's stopped. I sprint full tilt through the mud, sliding over the rocks and grass. Down the hillside now to the driveway. I'm almost there. My fingers are numb. Everything aches. I fumble with the set of keys. There are so many in the bunch. I try different ones in the lock, shifting through the knotted and curled metal.

Finally, the gate unlatches. I heave it open, my muscles burning. The metal makes this awful scraping sound on the concrete, but I'm not stopping now. I'm not slowing down.

I rush out on the empty road, chest heaving. Looking to the left. To the right. Scanning the horizon in both directions in hopes that I see a car, some passerby, anything. But I'm in the middle of nowhere. We didn't see anyone else on the road yesterday. Why should now be different?

I run in one direction, not giving up. My breath comes out in ragged gasps. I stare at the road, willing there to be someone to take us away from this place.

But there's nothing. No one. We're alone.

I keep running. *Please*, I think. *Give me something. Please.* But still, I'm the only one here. I let out a frustrated cry and look over my shoulder, and that's when I see them.

Headlights. Cresting a tiny hill.

I wave my hands. "Hey! *Hey!*" I scream, running towards the lights. I'm so focused on where I'm going I almost miss the body hunched on the side of the road.

Jackson.

He's curled over, trembling. It takes me a moment to realize who he is. My heart feels like it might burst. "Oh, God! Jackson. How'd you escape?"

I go to him. He raises a hand and doesn't look at me. A car comes into view. The headlights grow larger. Brighter. Washing over me.

"We're going to get you out of here," I say. "Don't worry. We're almost home."

We've done it, I think. *We've survived.* When I step closer, Jackson turns sharply away.

"Let me see. Can you move?" I ask.

He shivers. "I'm fine. Help El."

"But how did you get over the gate?" My head pounds, exhaustion setting in. I wave my hands at the car. Jackson breathes in short, deep gasps. His whole body shakes. Why won't he look at me?

"You seen Beth?" he asks, his voice quiet and calm. "Been looking for her."

The question throws me off guard. I shake my head, unsure of how to answer him. He knows what happened to Beth. We all know. The car is almost here.

"Must have been tired of waiting," he says, still crouched away from me.

I study my brother's skin, noticing he's not that dirty, not after what we've been through. There should be mud and blood on him, but Jackson's barely damp, whereas I'm soaked through. "Jackson…" I say, not sure where to start. "You did get over the gate. Right?"

There's a heavy moment. He stops shaking.

Finally, he turns to me and my chest tightens. His jaw is broken and lop-sided. Bloody gashes crisscross his face.

"Oh, Jackson," I say.

His eyes lock with mine. After awhile, his face contorts, his lips stretching upwards, and I realize he's actually smiling at me, though it's a grotesque display in his current state.

The car pulls closer, flashing its lights. I wave at the driver, but when I glance back to my brother, he's gone. The car beeps. A man opens the driver's side door, his forehead knotted in worry.

"Miss? Are you okay? Miss?" The man keeps talking, his lips moving, but my mind's reeling. All I can do is look at the space where Jackson once stood.

10

In the sparse hospital waiting room, I sit next to an old lady muttering to herself about how she's late, late, always late. Across from me is a man without any teeth. He chomps down on his gums like he's chewing grass. My arm throbs from where the dog bit me. There's a butterfly bandage that itches the corner of my mouth.

I stare at the floor, trying to process the past 24 hours. Bruises are already forming on my arm. My shins and thighs are soft with pain. *But you're alive*, I think. *You survived.*

"Angela?" A round nurse looks at me expectantly. "It's okay to see him now."

I rise to my feet. "Thanks," I mumble, a spike of pain shooting through my cheek. I head down the long corridor. Fluorescent lights flicker overhead. Everything about this place is gray: the walls, the food, the lights…

A heavy-set man in a hospital gown wanders ahead of me. He takes one step forward and then a few steps back. At first I think he's one of the residents, but on closer inspection, his flesh is pale and his eyes are vacant, not of this world. I keep still as the stench of death fills my nostrils.

Cautiously, I slip past the wandering apparition and make my way through a door on the right. Elliot's propped up in bed, his leg elevated. Bandages cover his body and tubes and wires probe and poke his arm. A BP monitor chirps in the corner. He slowly turns his head to look at me. A frail smile spreads across his lips.

"Hey," I say, caught off guard by how he's hooked up to so many machines.

"Hey you," he replies. I tiptoe closer, afraid I'll somehow disturb his recovery. We don't say anything. Elliot reaches for me. I place my hand in his and give it a good squeeze. We stare into each other's eyes. There are little flecks of green in his, and seeing this again, the random details of this boy's life, levels me in a way I can't describe.

Because we're the last ones standing. We're still here.

Walking out of the recovery room, orderlies pass me by, their eyes just as dull as the departed. My mind drifts back to Jackson, seeing him on the side of the road with that mutilated grin on his face. Has he found Beth now? Is he in a better place? I guess dead or alive, we're all slaves to something.

At the end of the corridor is a long line of vending machines. Silver sides. Double-stick padding. I walk over and browse the chocolate and sugar coated options, this mundane action calming me. To be honest, I'm not even hungry, but after not eating since yesterday I feel like it's something I should do.

My phone vibrates in my pocket. I place it gingerly to my ear. My father breathes on the other side. I can hear him crying. "Dad? Are you there?"

His voice catches in his throat. Short, staccato breaths punctuate the silence. He tries to speak, but can't. I think about how I just saw Jackson, and how I can never explain to my father that there's a part of him still with us. "Dad, I'm sorry I missed your calls."

His voice stops and starts. "Ange. My God. Are you all right?"

I tell my father what he wants to hear, that I'm well taken care of, that I'm safe. Punching in a code to the vending machine, it whirs in front of me. The mechanism turns, and I'm comforted, watching the candy bar fall down with a *plunk*. At least there's some order to the universe. At least I can press a button in a grey hallway and know a small rectangular piece of chocolate is going to plop down a metallic chute.

"There's nothing you could've done," I say. "Jackson's… No one could have known." A car horn blasts through the phone. My father curses. Tires squeal. "Dad. Please. *Please* don't speed."

I feel like I should comfort him, tell him everything's going to be okay, but I never believed people when they said that to me. I was never the reassuring one. Not like my mother. Not like Jackson, even though I could never tell if Jackson was faking or not.

Bending down to retrieve the candy bar, I hear that ringing noise again. It's dull, wafting in and out. I hold my breath. Something's different about this time though. I'm not afraid. Not like before.

"Ange, are you still on the phone?" my father asks.

I focus on the ringing and it lessens in intensity. A small rush of excitement tingles through me. Ringing means I'm not alone. Sure enough, over my shoulder, Jackson looms. I catch a glimpse of his face in the glass reflection. "I'm here," I say. "I am. Please don't cry."

"I'm getting there as fast as I can, Ange. I'll be there. Soon. Soon."

"Okay, Dad. Just don't rush. Okay?"

"You shouldn't have to deal with this. It's too much. No one should have to deal with this."

My brother sidles next to me, perusing the vending machine options. "Don't worry," I say into the phone. "I have someone with me."

"Not the same though. It's not family."

My eyes meet with Jackson's. I feel elated and sad all at once.

"I'm almost there," my father says. "I'm coming for you. It's just you and me now."

"Okay," I reply.

Something wet trickles down my nose. I concentrate, and the blood slows. Wiping it away with the back of my hand, for the first time in my life, it occurs to me that this curse my mother gave me might just be a gift. Something useful. Something good. My father keeps talking. He tells me about the arrangements we have to make. He doesn't know how he's going to pay for any of this. I can feel the stress in his voice, the weight of the situation eating away at him.

My mother used to say there were moments in your life that defined you. Moments that you knew, while you were living them, you would never forget. Looking at Jackson's reflection, hearing the panic in my father's voice, I know that this is one of them. A turning point. A new beginning.

I will never be alone again. I will never be anyone's victim. A deep warmth overtakes me, and it's the best high, knowing we are never, ever on our own. Even in death. I want to shout what I know to the grey sky. I want to go back and kiss Elliot. All these people in the world, waiting and wishing to connect with their loved ones. They can't, but I can. I can help them. And knowing this, knowing I have some sort of worth, some sort of purpose in this life, lifts my spirits in a way I never thought possible. I take my candy bar and walk back down the hall. Without even looking behind me, I know my brother's still there.

ABOUT THE AUTHOR

Eva Konstantopoulos hasn't been able to sleep in a very long time. Currently, she lives and writes in Southern California.

Made in the USA
Middletown, DE
21 October 2023

41206753R00090